D0332809

RUGBY

HEROES

GERARD SIGGINS

LIBRARIES NI
WITHDRAWN FROM STOCK

THE O'BRIEN PRESS
DUBLIN

First published 2018 by
The O'Brien Press Ltd,
12 Terenure Road East, Rathgar,
Dublin 6, Ireland
D06 HD27
Tel: +353 1 4923333; Fax: +353 1 4922777
E-mail: books@obrien.ie.
Website: www.obrien.ie

ISBN: 978-1-84717-997-5

Copyright for text © Gerard Siggins 2018
Copyright for typesetting, layout, editing, design
© The O'Brien Press Ltd

All rights reserved.
No part of this publication may be reproduced
or utilised in any form or by any means,
electronic or mechanical, including photocopying,
recording or in any information storage
and retrieval system, without permission
in writing from the publisher.

8 7 6 5 4 3 2 1
21 20 19 18

Printed and bound by CPI Group (UK) Ltd, Croydon, CR0 4YY
The paper in this book is produced using pulp from managed forests.

Published in:
DUBLIN
UNESCO
City of Literature

DEDICATION

To Peter and Nuala, great friends

ACKNOWLEDGEMENTS

Thanks to my family for all their support and encouragement. As ever, the brilliant editing of Helen Carr has helped me see this book into your hands. She has been a true Rugby Hero over the six books of the series.

CHAPTER 1

CHRISTMAS was Eoin's favourite time of the year. He had a stack of memories of joyful mornings when he benefited from being the only child – and grandchild – in his family.

As he stretched out in his bed and lifted his legs over the side he wondered what delights would be under the tree for him this year.

Since he had started to do well at rugby there was no point asking Santa or his family for the usual presents of sportswear, as his wardrobe was stuffed solid with jerseys and tracksuits in both Leinster blue and Ireland green.

He had dropped a few hints about how he missed cycling since he'd outgrown his bike, and how good it might be to help him vary his fitness training. While he had been rested during the Mini World Cup he had borrowed a bike to get around the university campus and enjoyed the freedom it gave him.

Although it felt like so long ago, it was only a week or so since Ireland had won the final and Eoin had helped solve the mysterious theft of the William Webb

Ellis Cup – with a little help from the man after whom the cup was named. Thinking of those days brought him back to the exciting moments of glory when Sam Farrelly had scored the winning try and Charlie Bermingham had lifted the trophy over his head. He felt a warm fuzzy glow rush through him and he jumped up from the bed, lifting an imaginary World Cup over his own head and taking the applause of the crowd.

He had been surrounded by newspaper reporters and cameramen after the game, but the Garda detectives had told him it was important he didn't say anything about the crime or the operation to recover the trophy as it might prevent the thieves from being sent to prison. Eoin was happy to keep quiet as he hated being the centre of attention anyway.

The IRFU was particularly delighted with his detective work, however, and he was chuffed when he got down home to Ormondstown for the holidays to find a letter of thanks from its president. He was even happier when he noticed that the paperclip on the top of the page was attached to four thin pieces of cardboard: 'Ireland versus England at Aviva Stadium, Saturday 30 March' was all Eoin bothered to read before he whooped with delight and rushed to show his mum.

He'd decided to say nothing to his grandfather, but

instead slipped one ticket inside the pair of socks he always bought him for Christmas. That would be an excellent present!

Eoin dressed quickly and rushed down the stairs as quickly as he had every Christmas morning since he'd been able to walk. He popped his head into the kitchen, where his parents were already hard at work preparing breakfast and dinner.

'Happy Christmas, Mam, Happy Christmas, Dad!' he smiled. 'I wonder what's under the tree for me?'

He hugged his parents and handed over his gifts to them, before crossing to the sitting room, where a shining bicycle awaited him.

'Just what I wanted!'

'Why don't you run over to see Dixie?' suggested his mother. 'He's been on the phone already so he's up and about. Tell him your dad will collect him about one o'clock.'

'That would be great – but are you sure you don't want a hand peeling sprouts?' asked Eoin.

'Does the great detective Sherlock Holmes peel sprouts?' asked his dad. 'No, run on there and see your grandad.'

Eoin winced at what his father had said – he really hated the attention he had got over the incident, and got particularly embarrassed when people called him a hero – but then he grinned gratefully and wheeled his bike out of the house, pausing to admire its perfect dark blue paintwork.

Eoin's grandfather, Dixie Madden, was once a great rugby player, and he had become Eoin's greatest supporter. He lived in a cottage nearby and Eoin called to see him every day he was home from boarding school.

'Hi, Grandad, merry Christmas to you,' Eoin called as he spotted the old man opening the curtains at the window.

Dixie lifted his hand in salute and moved to open the door.

'Well, was Santa Claus good to you?' he asked.

'Very!' replied Eoin, hopping off and pointing to his brand-new bike.

'Oh, that's a beauty,' smiled Dixie. 'Does she move well?'

'Like a dream,' replied Eoin. 'I got over here in about two minutes flat,' he pointed to his watch. 'I've never run it faster than five.'

'That's good news, you'll have that bit more time to

spend with me when you call over now,' Dixie chuckled.

'Dad says he'll call over at one o'clock,' Eoin said, as the old man ushered him inside.

'That will give us plenty of time to talk about rugby,' said Dixie. 'We will have to get that project of yours finished too.'

Eoin's face fell.

'Grandad… it's Christmas Day! You don't expect me to do school work today, do you?'

'Ah no, sure this isn't work at all,' laughed Dixie.

'Hmmm,' mused Eoin. 'It certainly sounds like it. What do you have in mind?'

'Well, your project is on the origins of rugby and William Webb Ellis – the chap whose trophy you discovered. But besides Ellis spending some time here as a boy, there's nothing about the early days of rugby in Ireland. So, well, I thought you'd like this…' said Dixie, handing Eoin a parcel. 'I've a few other presents for you, but this will be useful.'

Eoin tore open the wrapping and saw that it was a book on the history of the rugby stadium on Lansdowne Road. He riffled through the pages, catching sight of old players whose names Dixie had mentioned to him. His friend Brian, too, had told him about the stars he had seen play at the ground.

'Wow, thanks Grandad, this is excellent,' he grinned. 'I promise I'll start reading it tonight.'

Dixie laughed. 'Well, I don't expect you'll allow it to get in the way of the important Christmas things such as eating and watching TV...'

CHAPTER 2

After lunch, Eoin dished out his presents – socks and chocs – but he especially enjoyed seeing the delight on his grandad's face when he saw there was a surprise bonus tucked inside. They made plans to meet up before the game and have a full day's fun with his parents.

The rest of the day flew by, but over the evening several visitors arrived, and each set wanted to hear Eoin recount his adventure.

He was therefore delighted when the last of them left, and with a yawn he said good night and hauled himself upstairs.

Eoin was tired and happy as he lay down on his bed. He reached over and picked up the book Dixie had given him, and read through the early chapters before he decided it was time for sleep. He flicked on a few pages and was amazed to see there was a whole chapter on his friend Brian.

He had heard the story of the young Lansdowne player, and how he had lost his life, but it was still interesting to read about it in detail, and the book told him a lot more about Brian than the modest ghost had let on. Eoin read that Brian had been a seriously good prop, and had just been selected for the Leinster junior side to play Munster when he became the only player to lose his life playing on the ground. He grinned at how his friend had faced the same dilemma as he had in opting to play against his native province.

He studied the photo of Brian, amazed that he looked the same now as he had almost a century before. He felt a tinge of sadness that he wouldn't see his pal for a couple of weeks, and wondered what ghosts got up to over Christmas.

Eoin closed the book and nodded off quickly, sleeping deeply and soundly until a loud knock came to his front door early the next morning.

'Howya, Eoin!' came the call as he peered round the side of the curtain. 'Get down here and we'll go for a spin!'

Outside was his great friend and school-mate Dylan, and he was pointing at a shiny bicycle of the same make as Eoin's, although his was painted red.

'Santa got the rugby colours right, anyway,' chuckled Dylan as Eoin wheeled his own bike through the doorway.

Eoin was startled at what Dylan had noticed. Although Eoin was from Munster, he went to school in Leinster and had been selected to play for that province. It meant he got a bit of slagging thrown at him around Ormondstown, but he had got used to that and reckoned it was just some people's way of acknowledging his success. Still, he never wore a blue Leinster shirt around town, reckoning that might be just a little bit too provocative.

Dylan had no problem with wearing rugby shirts though, and was rarely seen in school or over the holidays without the red Munster shirt he had earned in the interprovincial championships the previous year. He was even wearing it today.

'I might repaint the bike green to keep them guessing,' laughed Eoin.

'But they'd think you were just being cocky about playing for Ireland,' frowned Dylan.

Eoin laughed. 'Yeah, you're right. Everyone has an opinion about me now that I've been on the TV news. I'll just paint it purple and hope nobody notices it's me cycling it.'

The pair rode around town twice, which didn't take very long. They stopped for a chat with Dylan's sister Caoimhe and her pals, who were out on their new bikes too.

15

'They'll have to put cycle lanes in Ormondstown soon,' laughed Dylan. 'Looks like everyone got a bike for Christmas.'

'I saw you in the paper for rescuing that trophy,' said Iris McCabe. 'You were very brave.'

Eoin blushed and laughed it off. 'I didn't do much, I was in the back of a Garda car when all the action happened.'

'The papers said you were a "brave schoolboy star",' chuckled Caoimhe. 'I cut it out for you in case you missed it.'

'Did you stick it in the scrapbook you have about him?' asked Iris.

Eoin and Caoimhe blushed, and Eoin changed the subject. 'I wonder is there anywhere we could buy locks for the bikes? I wouldn't leave them out around town without being chained up.'

'I'd say you'd be all right,' said Iris. 'Sure, everyone knows everyone in this town. No one would steal from their neighbours, would they?

CHAPTER 3

The school holidays, as usual, went by quickly. Eoin spent a couple of afternoons chatting with his grandad about his project, adding to it from his new book, and a couple more nights putting it all together.

He was happy he had completed it before he went back to school as it was one less thing he had to worry about. The next six months were going to be busy – Castlerock were mad keen to defend the Junior Cup he had helped them win the year before, and he had his Junior Certificate exams at the end of the school year. The mini World Cup had been a big distraction and he knew he was behind with his studies, which annoyed him. He knew he wasn't a top ten student but if he worked hard he could get good results.

He spent the last morning of the holidays putting together a timetable right up to the exams and was just finished when his mother told him the postman had a letter for him.

Eoin has glad of the distraction and skipped down the stairs two at a time. He was even happier when he saw that it was another letter with the words 'Irish Rugby Football Union' stamped in green along the bottom of the envelope.

'Maybe they're sending me more tickets for the England game?' he grinned at his mother.

But the letter had a different purpose entirely.

'*Dear Eoin Madden,*' it began.

'*The recent World Rugby Under-16 World Cup was an unqualified success, and we were delighted that you played an important part in Ireland's ultimate victory. The board of the Irish Rugby Football Union were so impressed by your team's efforts that it has approached other members of the Six Nations about setting up an Under-16 version of the championship. Four unions have agreed to take part.*

'*We appreciate that many of your team will be busy with Junior Cups and examinations, so we propose to run the event off in one week in mid-March. We will be back shortly with precise timings and fixtures, and hope you will make yourself available for selection by replying to this by email by 5pm next Friday.*'

Eoin jumped in the air in delight.

'They're having a Six Nations for Under 16s, Mam!'

he squealed. 'Looks like it will be around St Patrick's Day. It's around the mid-term break I think, too'.

'Are you picked?'

'No, but they've asked am I available. I should be OK to make the squad, maybe even start.'

Eoin made for the front door, but stopped.

'What's wrong?' asked his mum.

'I was going to cycle over to Dixie to tell him but I better get upstairs and start shifting around my timetable again. This makes a mess of my plans to come home and study that week.'

'Ah, that can wait. Run down and tell him, he'll be so delighted.'

Eoin grinned and dashed outside where he found his bicycle chained to the fence.

'Your dad got you a lock, the key is hanging inside the door there. You can't be too careful with a new bike,' his mother told him.

Eoin thanked her, unlocked his bicycle and sped over to Dixie's house. He checked his watch as he reached the gate and saw he'd knocked four seconds off his personal best for the journey.

Dixie was delighted at the news from the IRFU, and wrote the date in his new pocket diary. After a few minutes' chat Eoin explained he had to get back to his study plan and waved goodbye.

But as he mounted his bicycle, around the corner came Caoimhe and Iris, who were both crying.

'What's wrong, Caoimhe?' he asked.

'It's our bikes,' she replied. 'And Dylan's. They've been stolen – all of them.'

'Ah no, that's terrible,' gasped Eoin.

The girls stared at the chain hanging from his handlebars.

'My dad bought me a lock, otherwise I never would have thought of it,' Eoin said.

Iris, who looked more angry than upset, asked, 'Who would be stealing three bikes?'

'Five actually!' gasped Dylan, who had just jogged around the corner. 'I met the Savage brothers and they had two nicked from their back garden.'

'It's a total crime wave,' said Caoimhe, still sobbing.

'I'll have a look around the town,' suggested Eoin, hopping back onto his bike. 'I'll call down to your house if I see anything.'

Dylan nodded, and told him he'd check out the back alleys and the car parks in case they'd been hidden there.

'It's probably an organised gang, with a van, so be careful,' said Iris.

Eoin cycled away, taking a wide circle of the town

and coming back towards Dixie's house. Through a gap in the high wall, he looked towards the old Lubov mansion that had been the starting point for one of his adventures last summer. He was surprised to see a white figure walking up and down the steps of the house in an agitated state.

'Alex,' he whispered to himself.

He decided that this wasn't the time to renew his friendship with the ghost of the old Russian prince who had once played rugby for England.

He circled back to his grandad's house but, as he hadn't seen anything of the bike thieves, he decided to head home.

CHAPTER 4

oin spent the evening reorganising his schedule, making copies of his rugby project, and packing his kit for the term ahead. In earlier years his mother had filled the suitcase for him, but now she left him to make his own choices. He carefully laid out his favourite t-shirts and rugby tops, before finally cramming in the school uniforms wherever they would fit.

Conscious that he would be back at training the next day, he had a small portion of pasta before making one last call down to Dixie to say goodbye. The old man had got Eoin's Ireland shirt framed for him for Christmas and offered to do the same with the Leinster one for his birthday.

It was dark and as Eoin hadn't got around to buying a lamp for his bike, he put on his heaviest coat, stuffed the blue Leinster shirt into his pocket, and strolled down through the town with a hat and scarf keeping the biting wind at bay.

Dixie was tired, and ready for bed, but said he was looking forward to watching the international in Lansdowne Road. Eoin told him about the thefts around town and asked him had he seen anyone or anything out of the ordinary.

'No, nothing changes very much around here,' replied Dixie, as he searched through his memory. 'But there was one little thing that surprised me. I always go out for a walk past the Lubov house and I know exactly how the front gate hangs. This afternoon I noticed that it had been moved – opened fully and then closed because the grass was ripped and a rut had been cut in the mud. I examined the ground inside and it looked as if a car had been driven over it. I couldn't see anything so I walked on. But I can't imagine there's anyone living in there now – half the roof fell in a few months back.'

Eoin thanked his grandad and they said their good-byes. Eoin looked up the road towards the mansion as he left, wondering what had caused the tyre marks.

He walked quickly to Dylan's house and told him what Dixie had seen. He was also reminded of his glimpse of Prince Obolensky earlier in the day.

'Do you think all this has something to do with the bikes?' asked Dylan.

'Probably not,' said Eoin, 'but we're off to Dublin in the morning and if we don't check it out now we'll never know. I'm certainly not going to go in on my own, so get your coat on and let's head up to see if anything's happening. Bring a lamp if you have one.'

Dylan's face fell. 'I had one – but it went with the bike…'

CHAPTER 5

The mansion on the hill at the edge of town had been owned by a Russian gentleman who died many years before. Whatever relatives he had either didn't know about the house, or didn't care, and it had fallen into a bad state of disrepair due to vandals and the Irish weather.

Eoin and his friends had visited it a few times the previous summer but now, on a cold winter's night and with the roof missing, he had no intention of venturing inside.

The boys climbed over the gate, reckoning it would make less noise than swinging it open.

'Take it easy, Dyl,' hissed Eoin. 'Don't rush.'

Inside the grounds, and with the moon tucked in behind a cloud, Eoin struggled to make out the shapes of the out-buildings.

'I don't think there's any point going into the main house,' he whispered. 'If there's anyone here they would be parked around the back.'

He gestured to Dylan which way he thought they

should go. They struggled through the knee-high, wet grass, taking care to dodge around Mr Lubov's old sports car which had become rusted and overgrown by weeds.

Eoin looked up at the house, whose windows were long broken and was startled to see that Prince Alex was waving at him from the balcony upstairs, over the doorway.

'Do you see him, Dylan?' whispered Eoin.

'I do, that's Alex, isn't it?'

'Yeah, he seems to be pointing behind him into the room.'

'Maybe, but he could also mean to go around the back of the house,' suggested Dylan.

The moon flooded the grounds once again, allowing Eoin to get his bearings and work out the shortest route to the side of the house. He moved quickly into the shadows, fearful that they might be spotted out in the open.

Eoin spotted the tyre-tracks again, and followed them around the side of the mansion. He waited at the corner but, peering around it, he couldn't see anything out of the ordinary.

Dylan pointed to the clump of apple trees and suggested they make for them, but Eoin took another look up at the house and again spotted Alex pointing.

'He's saying to go to that building over there,' whispered Eoin. 'It looks like a barn, or a stable…'

Dylan darted across the yard to the largest of the outbuildings, peering in through where a plank had rotted and fallen away. He hurried back to Eoin.

'Alex was spot on. There's a white van in there, and two lads sitting in the front seat. There's a load of bikes stacked up against the wall, too, I'm nearly certain I saw my own Red Rover.'

Eoin grinned. 'Well look, we'll run down to the Garda station…'

Dylan interrupted. 'There's no one there at night anymore. You have to ring them – and they come from twenty miles away anyway.'

Eoin winced. 'My phone's dead.'

Dylan paused, thinking, before announcing that he had a plan.

'Look, those lads could be leaving tonight. It looks like they've cleared the town out of bikes and they're probably moving on somewhere else. We need to delay them – can you cause a disturbance out here and I'll sneak around the back and see what I can do?'

'Hang on, Dylan, be careful now. These are criminals we're dealing with – I don't want to be caught by them…'

'We'll be fine. Maybe if you throw a few stones up at what's left of the windows on the house and make as much noise as you can. Then scarper and ring the police from Dixie's. Leave the rest to me.'

Eoin sneaked back to the side of the house, and collected a few fist-sized stones. He tossed one towards a back window and listened as it made a satisfying tinkle. But nothing moved in the barn.

He chucked another, harder this time, and heard it crash through the window frame, but again, no reaction came.

He threw three more, in quick succession, clattering off the roof and crashing to the ground below to make quite a racket. Frustratingly, there wasn't a peep from the barn.

Eoin selected the biggest three rocks he had left, and decided to switch targets. He turned and aimed at the front door of the barn, and the first rock crashed noisily through the splintering wood. He followed it with a second, and was just about to throw the third when the door swung open and the headlights of the van broke through the darkness. Two men rushed out into the yard.

'Oi,' called one. 'Who's there?'

'Bloody kids,' roared the other. 'If I catch you…'

Eoin stayed as still as he could as the pair wandered

further away from the door, towards the big house. He wanted to delay them as much as possible, and when they both had their backs to him he lobbed the third, and heaviest, rock onto the roof of the mansion. It crashed through the tiles and fell into the room below. The thieves stared up at the house and Eoin took his chance to dash into the trees.

'Little brats,' roared the first thief. 'Should be in bed by now!'

Eoin made his way quickly out of the grounds, vaulting the gate and breaking into a trot as he hurried towards his grandfather's cottage. He was dismayed though, to find there were no lights on.

'Of course, Dixie was getting ready for bed when I was here an hour ago,' he muttered to himself. 'He won't be happy, but I'm sure he'll understand,' he added as he pressed the doorbell.

It took a second, and a third ring, before a light came on in the room Eoin knew was Dixie's bedroom. He waited at the front door as the hall light came on, and called through the glass at the old man.

'I'm sorry, Grandad – I have to use your phone. It's an emergency.'

The old man opened the door, looking very concerned.

'Eoin, my boy, come in, come in. Now what's all this about?'

Eoin explained as quickly as he could, and asked could he ring the Gardaí.

'Of course, of course, and ring your father as soon as you're finished with them. You can't be wandering the streets of Ormondstown late at night with gangsters on the loose.'

Eoin got through to a garda and told him quickly about the bike thefts – of which the gardaí were aware – and how he believed the stolen bicycles were being stored up at the old haunted mansion.

'And how do you know you haven't frightened them into leaving?' asked the garda, a question Eoin couldn't answer. 'And is your friend at the house still?' he added.

Eoin, again, was unable to tell him.

'But, Garda, can't you come quickly? There's two of them so bring reinforcements too.'

The garda said he would be there as soon as he could, and not to leave Dixie's house.

Eoin's dad arrived before the police and he was unhappy at what his son had been up to.

'Did you learn nothing from that thing up in Dublin?' he frowned. 'The best people to deal with criminals are the gardaí, not fifteen-year-old boys.'

The pair were waiting at the gate when the police car arrived, carrying two uniformed gardaí and two in plain clothes. Eoin quickly explained what had happened again, and drew a sketch of the lay-out of the buildings on one of the garda's notebook.

'Now stay here, and don't dare to come inside that gate again, no matter what happens,' said the senior policeman. 'Mr Madden, I'm relying on you to keep your son here.'

Kevin Madden nodded, and again said how sorry he was.

'No need to apologise,' said the garda. 'If this works out the lads will be heroes, but if it doesn't they'll have a few awkward questions to answer...'

CHAPTER 6

It was all over in less than five minutes. The gardaí moved in quickly and found the two thieves cowering in their vehicle.

The garda who arrested them warned them that they didn't need to say anything, but the two just kept gabbling and pointing at the mansion. What they said didn't make any sense to the guards.

'I wonder why they didn't make a run for it when they could?' asked another garda as they peered inside the van which was stacked full of mostly new bikes.

'There's why,' said a third, pointing to the rear tyres of the van, which were as flat as a pizza. 'Looks like someone has taken a knife to them.'

The guard shone her torch into the corners of the barn, but when she aimed the beam at the back of the building she was stunned as a red blur flew past her and raced out the back door.

'What was that?' she called.

'Is there a third man in the gang?' asked one of the detectives. He ran back out into the yard in time to see

the unidentified cycling object race around the side of
the house and out towards the main road.

The garda raced after it on foot, and was still puffing
when he got to the gate where he saw Eoin, his dad and
another boy wearing a blue rugby shirt standing on the
footpath.

'Did you see anyone come by here wearing a red
Munster top?' he asked.

The trio shook their heads.

'OK,' said the garda, puzzled. 'Well, I don't think it
was anything important. Probably another kid.

'I'm glad to report that we have captured the two
thieves with a van packed with the stolen bicycles.
They've been doing this for years across half of Ireland –
there might even be a reward for you in this. Or a medal.
But for now you need to get home to bed!'

The boys grinned, delighted that their plan had
worked and there had been a happy ending.

'The poor thieves look like they've seen a ghost.
They're terrified around there,' he told them, pointing
back at the house.

Eoin looked at the top floor of the Lubov mansion
and smiled as he saw a figure waving to him. He was all
white from top to toe, except for his chest on which he
wore a red rose.

As they walked back to Dixie's house, Dylan burst out laughing.

'That was a quick move, Eoin, fair play to you.'

Eoin smiled. He had realised Dylan was too conspicuous wearing a red shirt and as he had forgotten to give Dixie his Leinster one it made a perfect disguise to throw the garda off the scent.

'Now get that disgusting blue yoke off me before anyone else sees me in it,' laughed Dylan.

He rushed into Dixie's garden and retrieved the red bicycle he had thrown over the fence a few minutes before.

'Those bikes will be locked up as evidence for months,' he explained. 'I couldn't do without my Red Rover for that long.'

'Are you bringing it up to Dublin?' asked Eoin.

'I am indeed,' said Dylan. 'Are you leaving your blue thing behind?'

'Well, I hadn't thought of it, to be honest. I suppose if I do we'll have to go up in the train as there'd be no way of bringing one, let alone two bikes, in the car.'

Eoin looked at his dad.

'Well, if you're telling me you don't want me to spend

a whole day driving you up to Dublin and then driving home, I'd be delighted. Dylan, be ready by eleven and I'll drop your bags to the station. The pair of you can cycle over there on Red Rover and... Blue... berry.'

'Blueberry?' snapped Eoin. 'That's a totally uncool name for a bike. I'm not calling it that.'

'Well you better have a new one by tomorrow or I'll make sure the nickname "Blueberry" sticks,' laughed Dylan.

CHAPTER 7

It was hard to sleep after the excitement of the evening, and Eoin was still buzzing when he checked the time just after three o'clock. He got up for a drink of water and stood at the window looking out into the night.

Night-time was magical in Ormondstown: The deep darkness, the silence, and being able to wander down to a kitchen at any time were all things he missed about home since he had begun life in Castlerock College, the boarding school that had become home for the past four years.

He tiptoed back up to his room where his bags and suitcases were stacked just inside the door. Just before he slipped into bed he remembered Dixie's present, which he hadn't finished reading yet. He took it from the shelf and tucked it inside the Leinster kitbag.

His mother called him early and delivered a huge breakfast to the table when he sat down.

'You'll need a good meal inside you for the journey,' she insisted.

Eoin grinned and gave up any thoughts of starting a disagreement over the diet his rugby coach had asked him to follow. He enjoyed the mountain of bacon, eggs and sausages even more knowing that he would back training soon enough.

He made his farewells to his mother, and gave the Leinster shirt to Dixie who had called over to see him off.

'That was quite a to-do last night,' said his grandfather. 'I'm glad to hear it all worked out in the end – you gave me quite a fright when you called so late.'

Eoin apologised again, and promised he wouldn't do it again.

'We'll see you in the Aviva, Grandad, it's only a few weeks away now.'

Eoin's dad drove the luggage down to Dylan's house while he cycled behind. They loaded up Dylan's gear and the boys raced ahead to the railway station. When they got there Eoin's dad presented them with a serious problem.

'So how are you going to bring that stuff all the way over to Castlerock?' he asked, pointing at the stack of luggage on the footpath. 'It would be dangerous to try to cycle with it piled on your crossbar.'

The boys' faces fell. 'I suppose we could push the bikes?' suggested Dylan.

'It's about ten kilometres,' signed Eoin. 'It would take us hours.'

'And no taxi would take all that amount of stuff – and two bikes as well,' said Kevin.

They stared dejectedly at each other before Kevin offered to ring the school to see if anyone would be able to collect them.

On the train, the boys relaxed and chatted about the new year stretching out in front of them.

'I just can't wait for the summer,' said Dylan. 'For all the exams to be over and a chance to stay in bed all morning.'

'We've a good bit to go before we get there,' laughed Eoin. 'We've got the Junior Cup to win again, and I might get onto this Ireland team for the Four Nations, or whatever they're going to call it.'

'What's this?' bristled Dylan, who had been called up for the mini World Cup as last-minute cover when the Ireland team had an injury crisis. He was a very good winger but wasn't quite at the standard to be on the Ireland starting team.

'Oh, I must have forgotten to mention it,' blushed

Eoin. 'With all the fuss over the bikes and that... There's a competition for the mini World Cup teams – England, Scotland and Wales are coming over – I got a letter from the IRFU yesterday.'

'Fair play to you. I suppose there'll be no look-in for any of the lads on the fringe of the squad?'

'I don't know, Dyl. Why don't you ask?'

'Because they'd laugh me out of it, that's why. I suppose I'll just have to turn it on in the JCT and see where that gets me.'

'Exactly,' replied Eoin, 'They know who you are and what you can do. The injured lads must be OK now, but who knows what will happen in the next ten weeks. Train hard and play well, and there's no way they can ignore you.'

CHAPTER 8

r Finn met the boys at the station, and led them into the car park where he had left the school minibus. Dylan and Eoin lifted their bikes in between the seats and tucked their bags in around them.

'Your dad gave me a call,' said Mr Finn, a retired schoolmaster who had stayed around Castlerock to help out when needed. 'Happily, nobody else was using the minibus so here I am.'

The boys thanked him again, and Mr Finn asked how they had been since he had last seen them – the day they won the mini World Cup.

'Dixie was so thrilled that afternoon,' said Mr Finn, who was one of Eoin's grandfather's oldest friends.

'It was pretty special,' agreed Eoin. 'There's no doubt pulling on that green jersey, no matter at what level, gives you an amazing feeling.'

Dylan nodded and looked down. He had been part of the winning squad and had a winners' medal too, but because he hadn't got out on the field he didn't feel quite the same way as Eoin. He still felt uncomfortable about wearing the green jersey and would never do so in public like he did with his Munster shirt.

'Well, I hope you both get the chance to wear the Ireland Schools shirt next, then the Under 20s and who knows after that. But get a move on – Dixie and I won't be around forever, you know,' he chuckled.

Mr Finn was a careful driver and the journey back to school took far longer than they had expected, but the boys enjoyed it nonetheless. Mr Finn had taught history and he and Eoin discussed William Webb Ellis and the way he had been credited with inventing rugby.

'It's a very different sport these days,' said Mr Finn. 'I'd love to know what William would think of modern rugby.'

Dylan looked sideways at Eoin, who turned and looked out the window, trying not to laugh.

They arrived back at Castlerock to a welcoming party of Mr Carey, the rugby coach, and Mr McCaffrey, the headmaster.

'Ah, our heroes of the RDS,' called the head, invoking the venue where the mini World Cup was won.

'Well I didn't do much,' muttered Dylan.

'Nonsense,' said Mr Carey. 'This is a team game and you played your part by being ready to be called on when the team needed you. That's why they gave you all a medal.'

'And, of course, Eoin might be in line for yet another medal, I understand, a Garda medal,' said the headmaster. 'You do seem to get into all sorts of adventures. Perhaps it will all quieten down with your Junior Cert on the horizon.'

Eoin had been involved in a few scrapes in his earlier years in school too, and had every intention of doing what Mr McCaffrey suggested.

'Now, you can lock those bicycles in the boarders' bike-shed around the back,' said Mr Finn. 'I'll keep an eye on your bags.'

'And I'll meet you back here in an hour, if that's OK,' said Mr Carey. 'I want to have a chat about how we're going to win the Leinster Junior Cup.'

CHAPTER 9

The rugby coach had heard about the IRFU's plan for the Four Nations competition and was keen to work out how it would affect Castlerock's ambition to retain the Junior Cup.

'I've been talking to the Ireland coach and, as I understand it, the tournament comes just after the JCT semifinals and finishes a week before the final. But Neil expects to have a couple of training sessions with you before it kicks off.'

Eoin grimaced. He hadn't reckoned on that when he was revising his study plan.

'I see you're worried Eoin – and I appreciate that you're doing big exams this year. Which is why I asked you and Dylan here for this discussion.'

Dylan nodded.

'Last year was phenomenal, but there were no distractions,' Mr Carey started. 'This year we have a very strong, experienced Junior Cup squad, but at least three, maybe four, of you will be tied up with Ireland at the very wrong time as far as the school's team is concerned.'

Mr Carey stood up and walked to the window.

'Now, I am just as aware that you have your Junior Cert and will need to ensure you get all your work done, so I propose to reduce your rugby workload here in Castlerock.'

Eoin cleared his throat.

'I think it would be best for everyone if we took the captaincy away from you, Eoin. It will be one less burden for you to bear, and it will also allow me to leave you out of some games if I think we don't need you. For example, our first game next week is against a very weak school and I will be using that opportunity to give you and Charlie a rest, and I can try out some of the squad players.'

Eoin nodded, not sure how to react. He liked the idea of lessening his load, but he hated missing out on playing.

'OK, sir,' he started. 'But what if I my replacement does really well. Will I get back in?'

Mr Carey started to laugh, but checked himself. 'I'm sorry, I shouldn't have laughed there. But, Eoin, I can safely say you will get back into the team even if your replacement scores eight tries and kicks penalties from his own 22. You are one of the best players we have EVER had in Castlerock and I wouldn't be resting you if I thought we would need you or if there was any doubt you would come back.'

Eoin smiled weakly.

'So, what's going to happen?' asked Dylan. 'You're leaving Eoin and Charlie out for the first round of the cup? What about Rory and me?'

'Well…' started Mr Carey. 'I think there will be less danger of burn-out for you two. From talking to Neil he hasn't mapped you two into his first-choice fifteen and he's not sure even if you'll both make the squad. Rory only got in as scrum-half because of a couple of injuries and they're expected to be OK. I think it's the same for the wingers.'

Dylan's face fell.

'I'm sorry to be the bearer of bad news,' said the teacher. 'But…'

'That's OK,' snapped Dylan. 'I didn't expect to get back in, but I thought Neil might have explained it to me.'

'What I was going to say,' went on Mr Carey, 'was that although this may seem like bad news to you, there is a silver lining.'

'What?' asked Dylan, mystified.

'Well, I have had a good chat with the other coaches, and with Mr McCaffrey, and we have decided that you would be the perfect choice to captain Castlerock in place of Eoin.'

Dylan's jaw dropped. 'Me? Really?'

Eoin grinned. 'That's a great choice, Mr Carey. Dylan will be a brilliant captain.'

'I think so too,' said the coach. 'And just to be clear – he's captain for the whole season. Even if you come back into the side, Eoin, he's still the boss.'

CHAPTER 10

Dylan developed a new way of walking over the next few days. Like a pigeon, he thrust his chest forward and ambled with an exaggerated strut. Eoin was delighted that Dylan had been the one to take the honour of captaining the school from him, but was a little nervous that it had all gone to Dylan's head.

Eoin was chatting with Alan in the dormitory they all shared when Dylan walked in one afternoon.

'You know the way you're always in the middle when we walk around the yard,' he asked.

Eoin nodded carefully.

'Well now that I'm captain, maybe *I* should be in the middle?' said Dylan.

Eoin and Alan laughed.

'Are you serious? I've never noticed that before,' Eoin said.

'Yeah, it makes us look as if we're your, I don't know… your disciples?' said Dylan.

'And now you want me to become yours?'

'Well… it's just that I'm more important around here

now and I want to make sure everyone knows about it.'

Eoin waved him away. 'Ah, Dyl, you're the captain, and you'll be great. You don't have to use it to make yourself seem more important. Just relax.'

But Dylan wouldn't relax, and stormed off in a huff.

Rory popped his head around the door. 'What's with Dylan?' he asked. 'He stormed past me in the corridor – he totally blanked me.'

'I know – he's being a bit big-headed about being made captain. He'll get over it as soon as something goes wrong.'

But nothing went wrong in the first game, against Curleytown High. The school was playing in the Junior Cup for the first time and were overwhelmed by Castlerock, who scored twelve tries.

Mr Carey had told Eoin and Charlie to use the afternoon to study, and both were bent over their books when Dylan came whooping up the corridor after the game.

'FIVE TRIES,' he roared.

'I thought it was twelve?' said Eoin. 'One of the First Years came by to tell us a while ago.'

'Twelve? Nah, that's what the *team* got,' Dylan replied. 'Five is what Dylan Coonan got. FIVE! They say it's a school record in the Junior Cup, maybe even in the competition as a whole. What do you think of that?'

'Well done, that's nice for you,' replied Eoin. 'But the important thing is that the school got through to the next round. Who else played well?'

'Eh… well I didn't really notice,' Dylan shrugged. 'Richie Duffy wasn't much use at the kicking – I think he only converted the ones in front of the posts, and he even missed one of those. He scored a couple of tries I think, and Páidí got one too…'

'OK, well that was great. Who do we have in the next round?'

'Ligouri College again,' Dylan replied. 'They're pretty rubbish this year and I think Carey will leave you rest again. All right, get back to your books there. I have to go sign a few autographs for the First Years.'

Eoin frowned as Dylan left. He felt uncomfortable with players taking credit for their own performance in what is always a team game. You can only play well if the players you are depending on to get the ball to you – and to protect you when you have it – play well too. Being there to take the last pass and having the legs to get you over the try-line was an important role, but it was no more important than any other.

But that was Mr Carey's problem and one he would have to impress upon Dylan and anyone else who thought otherwise.

Eoin dived back into his French irregular verbs – rugby would have to take the back seat for a while.

CHAPTER 11

While Eoin was allowed to miss matches by Mr Carey, he wasn't allowed to miss any training sessions, and he kept fit by doing extra running and exercises on his own. He ended every day by running a couple of laps of the inside wall of the school, a circuit he often broke by stopping at the Castlerock landmark known as The Rock.

The huge stone, which sat beside a tiny stream, was hidden by bushes and was where Eoin's ghostly friend Brian Hanrahan was often to be found. Eoin sat on The Rock and sipped from his water bottle as he awaited Brian's arrival.

It was quite a surprise when two other ghosts arrived, spirits he had encountered in his earlier adventures but not seen since.

'Kevin, Dave,' he saluted them, 'What has you back in Castlerock, and on such a cold, dark night too.'

'I don't feel the cold much these days,' grinned Dave Gallaher, a legendary All Black who had been killed on the battlefields of Flanders during World War One.

'I like the atmosphere out here in the school,' admitted Kevin Barry, an Irish rebel who had been executed during the War of Independence. 'I like checking out the rugby training – it's very different to when I played back in Belvedere College.'

'It's a blooming totally different sport!' chuckled Dave. 'I honestly don't recognise a lot of what's going on, but I suppose these are different times and the youngsters seem to be enjoying it anyway.'

'Yeah, I've seen a few films of old games, back in the 1920s and '30s, and it looks a lot slower,' suggested Eoin.

Dave frowned at that. 'I'm not surprised with the heavy boots we had to wear, and the ball always rock hard when it got wet!' he argued. 'Men were a bit smaller in those days – but we were definitely tougher!'

'Anyway, so the reason why we're here…' started Kevin.

'… Is a complete mystery to us too,' added Dave.

'When you're, you know… dead,' went on Kevin. 'Well, time passes in different ways and in different places. Sometimes you get summoned to a place when someone thinks of you, but after all my family and friends had died then that stopped happening very often. Other times, it can be a ghost that calls you – someone you knew when you were alive, or like now, who you only met after you were dead. I bumped into Dave here tonight and we reckon that it must have been Brian who sent out word that we were needed. Have you any idea if there's anything going on?'

Eoin shook his head, puzzled. 'No, there's nothing out of the ordinary at all. That's a bit strange about Brian – and there's been no sign of him either.'

He stayed chatting about rugby to the pair for ten minutes – Kevin never tired of telling him how he once scored a famous try for his school in a cup semi-final at Lansdowne Road – before Eoin mentioned that he had been playing for Ireland and had even beaten Dave's famous All Blacks in the mini World Cup final.

'The baby Blacks? That's an amazing result,' said the former New Zealand captain who had been born in Ireland. 'I bet none of that team will ever be picked again.'

With no sign of Brian, Eoin bade the pair goodnight and told them he'd call back at the same time tomorrow. He jogged slowly back across the field and looked up at the night sky. It was a bright and almost full moon, but just as he reached the school a huge black cloud raced across the sky and appeared to swallow the moon whole. Eoin shivered and ducked inside the front door.

CHAPTER 12

ut Brian wasn't there the next night, nor the one after, and his ghostly friends became a little concerned.

'I don't know what we should do,' said Dave, 'I wonder is he in any sort of trouble?'

'Hard to know what could be worse trouble when you're already dead,' joked Kevin, but Eoin was starting to get worried about his friend.

'Well, I'll keep coming back here every morning and every night,' he said, 'It would be great if you could too.'

'I'll be here,' said Dave, 'Brian's a good bloke and I'm always keen to help out a fellow Irishman.'

The trio resolved to meet up again the following evening.

Next day was the second round of the Junior Cup, and although Mr Carey told Eoin he would rest him, he asked him to come along and watch the match.

Eoin had a keen eye for rugby tactics and Mr Carey

often compared notes and took his views into account about selection and switching positions.

Ligouri College played on the banks of the river close to Lansdowne Road, and Eoin decided to come early to the game and visit the stadium in case Brian was around.

He parked his bicycle beside the souvenir shop, which was close to the entrance to the tunnel that ran under all the seated areas, allowing buses, ambulances and other vehicles to get around inside the ground. While the security guard was busy checking one of the delivery vans, Eoin ducked inside and made his way towards the dressing room areas.

He was fortunate not to meet anyone on the way, because he hadn't worked out a story that would give him any real reason to be there. Eoin was also fortunate that he knew his way around – since that first visit on a school tour he had been here three times as a player and on several other occasions to watch matches.

He smiled as he remembered his first visit as a specta- tor when he wore with pride the red shirt of Munster that his grandfather had given him. He couldn't wear that shirt anymore, not just because it was too small, but because he was now a fully-committed Leinster player. He still loved his native province, and secretly cheered when they won a big game, but he couldn't let that get in the way of his commitment to the Blues.

'At least there won't be any more interpros this year,' he thought, 'It will all be the green shirt from now on.'

Eoin paused and checked his bearings. He wanted to find the treatment room where he had first met Brian, but as he had been lost when he happened upon the old player's spirit, he couldn't remember how to get there. Nothing looked familiar and, after trying several doors, he gave up.

He rambled back through the service tunnel, annoyed that he hadn't been able to find his friend. He skipped over a large puddle, and blinked as he came out into the sunlight.

He stopped at the souvenir shop for an ice cream, checking out the new-style Ireland shirts and wondering would he get the chance to wear one himself. As he left to walk across the bridge to Ligouri College he glanced down the slope into the underground car park where he just caught a glimpse of a rugby shirt, a flash of black, red and gold.

It shouldn't have been a surprise to see the famous colours of the Lansdowne club, who had been one of the earliest clubs and played on the ground for nearly 150 years. But Eoin knew only one person who wore that shirt, and he had been searching for him for the past hour.

CHAPTER 13

Eoin paused, waiting for a car to exit the car park.
He made his way down the slope and adjusted his eyes, looking left and right into the darkened corners.

'Brian!' he called, but there was no sound or movement in reply.

He wandered deeper into the car park, eventually reaching the back wall. Exasperated, he turned to go back to the entrance and was irritated when he stepped in a puddle and the water seeped in over the sides of his shoe.

'Bummer, that was a deep one!' he grimaced. 'I hope I can borrow a pair of socks at the game.'

Having reminded himself of the main reason he was in the area, he hurried up the slope and across the bridge to watch Castlerock's second-round fixture. His school were already 7-0 up, and from the way Dylan was strutting around he presumed the stand-in captain had scored the first try.

He took off his soaked sock and joined Mr Carey on the touchline. Alan was there with a clipboard and stopwatch, wearing his Leinster beanie.

'Sorry I'm late, sir, I cycled in and was a bit confused by the one-way streets,' said Eoin.

Mr Carey nodded and pointed out onto the field.

'Nothing to worry about here,' he said. 'They're so weak they're making Richie Duffy look good at out-half.'

Duffy had made Eoin's life miserable when he first came to the school, but by standing up to him Eoin had ensured he never bullied him or his friends again. Eoin had taken his place at Number 10 on the school team and never lost it.

Duffy was a good player, but not anywhere near as good as Eoin had become. He didn't put in the long hours of practice that Eoin did, and it showed with his kicking, which was sloppy and rarely found the target.

Eoin looked at Alan's clipboard and thought. He pointed out to Mr Carey what Duffy was doing wrong with his place kicks, but the teacher grinned and told him not to worry about Duffy.

'This will be his last start of the season,' he told him. 'I want you back for the quarter-finals and hopefully all the way to the final over there,' he added, pointing over his shoulder at the stadium.

Eoin spent most of the first half with Alan, who had

shown a great interest in compiling statistics about the team's plays and how often a player touched the ball and what he did with it. Mr Carey told him he found it useful so Alan persisted with it.

'It's funny how you watch a game differently when you're counting mistakes,' said Alan. 'Some guys I thought were good players are knocking on three or four times every game, and some guys just never look for the ball.'

Eoin grinned. 'I'd keep that sort of information to yourself. It's a sure-fire way to make yourself unpopular for that to get out.'

'It's not all negative,' said Alan. 'I've been taking notes on tries and kicks for a couple of years now and I've worked out the most effective moves to lead to a score.'

Eoin's eyes widened. 'Really?

'Yeah," replied Alan. "That switch kick you do when you shape at kick-off towards the packs and then snap it out to the wing? I don't know why you don't use that more often. You've tried that four times over the last two years, and scored three tries from it, including in the World Cup final. I'll remind you next time you need a try."

Castlerock had clinched their place in the next round by half-time, when they led by more than twenty points. Dylan scored two more tries after the break to ensure a 44-0 win.

'That's eight tries in two games,' he chuckled later in the dormitory as he stretched out on his bed. 'Do you reckon that's a Leinster record?'

Eoin shrugged as he tossed his dirty socks into the laundry bag. 'I wouldn't know, maybe you should ask Alan when he gets back from study.'

'What's up with you?' snapped Dylan. 'Are you not happy I scored a hat-trick?'

'Of course I am,' Eoin replied. 'It's just that you seem more interested in your *own* performance than the *team's*.'

Dylan glared back at him. 'That's rubbish.'

'Well then, how come you never asked me was I happy that the team won? And last time it was all "five tries" this, and now it's "hat-trick" that.'

Dylan bowed his head and left the room.

Eoin sighed, unsure if he had done the right thing. But one glance at the clock and the realisation that he had to have his maths homework complete in the twenty-five minutes before lights-out ensured he quickly forgot all about Dylan and rugby.

CHAPTER 14

Eoin swung by The Rock on his morning run, but there was no sign of any of his other-world friends. He paused for a swig from his water bottle and ran on, but as he passed the rugby pitch he was astonished to see Richie Duffy out practising his goal kicks. Mr Carey must have had a word with him, but as he was unlikely to play again it seemed like a waste of time. Still Eoin had to admire Duffy's commitment – practice time was never wasted time.

Because of the new Four Nations competition it was decided by the authorities to get schools fixtures over early, and Castlerock's quarter-final against Sandycove School was only three days away. Eoin went along to the training session after school and Mr Carey asked him to take his place as first choice out-half.

'Thanks a lot, Duffy and Hickey,' the coach said, 'we see you both playing an important role as this competition goes on, but right now we're bringing back Madden and Bermingham for the Sandycove game.'

Duffy glowered at the edge of the group, but he couldn't

really complain. With their star players, Castlerock were as good a JCT as any school in the province, maybe even the country. The rest of the team knew they had a good chance to collect winners' medals in the Aviva in a few weeks, but that chance was an awful lot greater with Eoin and Charlie back in the team.

Eoin slipped easily back into his usual position outside Rory, and the deep understanding between them was obvious after a few minutes. Dixie had once told Eoin that a strong 'spine' was vital for a good rugby team – from full back, through the half-backs up to the No. 8 and hooker. These were the pivotal roles in the team and the most talented players should play there. Eoin saw that Dixie spoke a lot of sense and it was obvious to everyone that having Charlie at Number 8, and Rory and Eoin as half-backs was a massive advantage for Castlerock, and the trio dictated almost every move and action.

But that didn't go down well with the captain-in-name perched out on the wing.

The three discussed one move as a scrum formed, but as Eoin hurried back to his position he spotted Dylan jumping up and down on the touchline.

'*I'm* supposed to be the captain,' Dylan grumbled at the next break in play. 'You and Charlie have taken over.'

'Ah, Dylan, it's only a training session and we're just trying something different. With you out on the wing its awkward.'

'OK, but call me over next time you want to make any changes,' Dylan snapped before turning and trotting back out to his position.

Eoin shrugged his shoulders and sighed.

The game against Sandycove was played on the Leinster branch pitch in Donnybrook, and Eoin loved getting the chance to play in a 'real' stadium where the grandstand towered above, packed with supporters.

These games also saw the arrival of the 'old boys', former pupils of Castlerock who came along to support the school's rugby teams in big games. Many had been at school many years before, but the noisiest were those who had left in recent years and were now college students. They delighted in loud roars of support and singing rude songs about the teachers.

Eoin grinned as he heard Mr McCaffrey's name being chanted, but when he heard the referee call the teams into position he blocked out everything that was going on outside the whitewashed lines.

Sandycove weren't a bad side, and were able to compete with Castlerock in the scrums and line-outs. But they didn't have the flair of the back unit marshalled by Eoin.

With Charlie and Rory controlling the speed of the ball coming to him, Eoin was free to unleash the plays that he and Mr Carey had worked on in training, and which owed a lot to the ideas Eoin had picked up at the Leinster and Ireland camps.

Eoin was much more aggressive in his running than Richie Duffy, and two of his breaks set up tries for Charlie who knew there would always be crumbs to be had by staying close to the shoulder of his out-half.

Castlerock led 17-0 at half-time, which should have made everyone happy, but there was one grumpy face as Mr Carey handed out the slices of orange.

'We need to bring the backs more into the game,' growled Dylan. 'We could catch frostbite out there on the wing.'

Mr Carey, and the rest of the team, looked shocked.

'I think we've been very effective in the way we have played so far,' the coach replied, carefully. 'There has been plenty of running and passing too, perhaps you have just been unlucky not to get much ball, Dylan.

'And anyway, the important thing is that,' he added,

pointing at the electronic scoreboard that blinked out the crucial numbers in bright red.

CHAPTER 15

Eoin wasn't impressed with Dylan's display of self-ishness, and his attempt to somehow blame Eoin for keeping the ball away from the backs. He certainly wasn't going to change his plans just because his pal was feeling a little chilly.

Once Mr Carey was finished Eoin headed for half-way and threw a few blades of grass in the air to check which way the wind was blowing. He glanced over at Alan who was wrapped up in what looked like two coats, two scarves and his woolly Leinster beanie. The team-stats man had his clipboard, but Eoin wondered what he could possibly be writing as he gripped the pen in his gloved fist as if he was carrying a dagger.

'Time for that thing we were talking about,' Alan called out, waving his clipboard.

Eoin grinned, and took a step back to look around the whole pitch, checking mostly where his left winger was.

As soon as the referee sounded the whistle, Eoin shaped to kick the ball between the converging groups of forwards on the right-hand side of the pitch, but at the last moment he pivoted on his standing foot and switched to face left. He had practised the move many times, and knew it was high-risk. The first time he had tried it he fell over and the ball went loose and cost his team a try.

But this time he executed everything perfectly. He could feel the hairs prickle on the back of his neck as he twirled around, and he got a surge of delight as his boot connected perfectly with the ball. Up it rose, aimed perfectly to hang above the Sandycove 22-metre line until his left winger could arrive to collect it.

However, Eoin's perfectly executed plan came to nothing. The Castlerock left-wing – Dylan – arrived far too late to make any attempt to catch the ball, and his opposite number gathered easily and moved the ball inside to build a platform to attack once more.

Eoin glared across at Dylan, who had his hands on his hips.

'Why didn't you tell me what you were going to do?' Dylan roared.

Eoin turned away, keen to get back in the game and unwilling to get involved in any debate with Dylan. He could have given him some signal, but that might have given the game away to Sandycove. Dylan should have been ready for anything and quicker to react.

Sandycove soon lost possession and Mikey O'Reilly nipped over for a third try, which killed off their resistance. Mr Carey made several changes and took Eoin off with twenty minutes left.

Perhaps sensing the tension between Eoin and Dylan, Richie Duffy suddenly changed from Eoin's more measured approach and began flinging the ball out to the backs at every opportunity. It meant Dylan got more chance to run with the ball, but the sloppy passing worried Mr Carey. A breakaway try for Sandycove proved his worries correct, but Dylan still came off the field with his arms in the air thanks to a last-minute run and touchdown under the posts.

'Brilliant try, Dyl, is that nine tries in the competition now?' asked Duffy with a sneaky grin on his face.

'Yeah, it's getting harder to score, but who knows who we'll select for the next game.'

Eoin snorted. He wasn't being cocky about it, but he knew there was no chance he would be dropped, no matter what Dylan thought.

Dylan's head turned and he glared at Eoin, but bit his lip.

'Nice try, Dyl,' Eoin offered.

'Thanks, it's good to get the chance to run sometimes,' he snapped back.

Eoin shrugged and went to shake the hands of the Sandycove boys.

CHAPTER 16

Eoin didn't have time for drama this term. There was a serious amount of homework to be done, and study when that was finished. He also had to fit in a couple of half-hour rugby sessions on his own every day, which comprised a morning jog and kicking practice after school or after training.

Rory had received some good news from Neil – he was no longer a stand-by player, but a full member of the international squad – but that wasn't good news for Castlerock.

Mr Carey was careful not to over-stretch Eoin, Rory and Charlie, and only invited them to one of the three JCT training sessions. But even with that, Eoin was exhausted.

'I just want to sleep all the time,' he told Alan one evening.

'But look, you've only two games – max – at the Four Nations, and two – max – with the school,' reasoned his friend. 'Four games of rugby and you can switch off all that and get into the books.'

'Well, when you put it like that…' mused Eoin, feeling instantly happier.

As it happened, Eoin's rugby schedule was even lighter than he thought. Next day came a letter from the IRFU, detailing the plan for the Four Nations, and when Eoin would need to report for duty.

As he read through the letter, the dates started whirring through his head as he fitted them into his mental calendar.

'Uh oh,' he mumbled. 'That's going to be a problem.'

Alan looked at him quizzically and peered over his elbow at the letter.

'Oh, bummer,' he squeaked, 'You start camp the day before the Junior Cup semi-final.'

'I know. And I'd be surprised if they allowed us out of camp to play in it.'

Eoin went looking for Rory and Charlie and found them both outside the staff room where they had gone to see Mr Carey.

'This is very disappointing,' said the coach, waving the IRFU letter. 'I'll give Neil a ring to see if there's any leeway – Dodder Woods have a player in the squad too, haven't they?'

But Neil wasn't having anything of Mr Carey's appeal. He told the coach politely that it was vital that the players joined the Ireland squad on that date, and that they focused fully on winning the Four Nations.

'What if one of them got injured?' Neil asked. 'At that late stage it would be disastrous to lose my first-choice out-half, scrum-half or captain'.

Mr Carey reluctantly agreed, and wished Neil well.

'No dice boys,' he told the three players. 'The only upside is that he regards you as his first picks, which is great news for you. We'll just have to beat Dodder without you.'

Eoin wasn't too disappointed at missing the semi-final. He knew the team would miss him, but still believed they had enough to win. After dinner, he slipped into his tracksuit and set off on a circuit of the grounds.

It was starting to drizzle, and as he was close to the small cluster of trees that surrounded The Rock, he ducked under their cover to escape the raindrops.

He parted the bushes to reach the stream and was startled to see he was not alone.

'G'day Eoin,' said Dave. 'Not an evening for a run, is it?'

Eoin grinned and looked behind the former All Blacks legend – following him through the bushes were Kevin Barry, Alex Obolensky and William Webb Ellis. All four heroes were united by their connection to rugby's past, but also by Eoin himself who had linked up with each of them over the past three years to help solve the mysteries that kept cropping up in his life.

'What has you all here?' asked Eoin.

'We're not sure,' replied Kevin, 'but we all got a strong message to get here as soon as possible.'

'Really?' asked Eoin, 'how does that work?'

'It is not like one of those texting messages,' replied Alex, 'It is like something that goes straight into your mind. It's how we communicate with other ghosts after we pass over into the after-life.'

'And you were all told to come here…?'

The quartet of spectres nodded.

'But where's Brian?' asked Eoin. 'Surely he….'

'Yeah, we reckon it was he who sent for us,' said Dave. 'We've been searching for him everywhere but with no luck.'

'I thought I saw him in Lansdowne Road a few days ago,' said Eoin. 'I even followed him into the under-

ground car park, but I couldn't find him. I hope he's
OK.'

The four ghosts told him they would keep looking,
and let him know how they got on.

CHAPTER 17

Mid-term break arrived, and Eoin spent the first few days studying as long as he could stay awake, broken up only by meals and his IRFU fitness programme.

On the Wednesday evening before the tournament started, Charlie, Eoin and Rory stacked their bags just inside the main entrance door to the school and waited for the mini-bus to arrive. Mr Carey had offered to drop them over to the hotel where they would be staying, close to the ground.

'Did anyone see the newspaper this morning?' asked Rory. 'There was a list of the squad and standby players. Dylan was down as being on standby – I don't think he knows that. He was very grumpy before breakfast when I was packing.'

Eoin shrugged. He was used to Dylan's moods, but he still didn't understand why his friend couldn't be happy for his friends when they did well – it wasn't as if it was his place they were taking.

Mr Carey helped them lug their bags aboard the bus

and waited as the headmaster came out to wish them well. A small crowd of junior boys had gathered too.

'Very best of luck boys, although you don't need any such thing. You have been such a credit to Castlerock this past year and brought such glory on the school. You don't owe us anything more, so just go out and enjoy this marvellous competition.'

The trio nodded and sheepishly took the congratulations. As they climbed into the bus Eoin noticed that Dylan had just come back from a run; he watched as Dylan bounded up the steps into the school without even a glance across at his team-mates.

Most of the Ireland squad – and their opponents – were already lounging around the lobby when Mr Carey finally found his way through rush hour traffic to the hotel.

'Eoooooinnnn!' came a call across the busy entrance area. Eoin struggled to work out who had hailed him, but when he heard it again coming from a huge grin wearing an Ulster shirt he knew instantly who it was.

'Paddy O'Hare! Great to see you,' he replied, delighted to meet his midfield team-mate from the Mini World Cup triumph.

The pair hugged before exchanging news and comparing notes on the action that was in store for them over the coming week.

'Neil was here earlier,' Paddy explained. 'He says we're training all day tomorrow, then a light run on Friday before we play Scotland on Saturday lunchtime.'

Eoin smiled. He remembered the World Cup and how Scotland had been pipped at the last moment – they would surely be gunning for revenge against Ireland.

'We have three days before the next game, against Wales, and then the last game against England – in the Aviva!'

'Really?' asked Eoin.

'Yeah, they're organising a whole day of games there – Scotland play Wales; then our game; then a women's international. It should be epic.'

'Three hard games in a week will be tough – I'd say Neil will be using the bench players big time,' suggested Rory.

'I expect so,' agreed Eoin. 'And for sure someone will get injured. Those Scots lads over there look like they might do some damage just by looking at us…'

CHAPTER 18

Training next day was difficult as it was a wild and windy day, but the team gelled quickly despite not having met up for months. After a hot shower the players were each given a new jumper and trousers by an IRFU bagman, the jumper carrying in gold thread the legend 'Ireland, Four Nations Under 16'.

'Swanky,' said Rory.

'This will get a few heads turning when we walk around Ormondstown, eh, Eoin?' laughed Roger Savage.

The players had a series of meetings with the Irish management and the tournament organisers before all the teams came together for a social event. Eoin and Paddy, with Sam Rainey, ducked into one of the corners of the hall and watched the rest of the players.

'There's poor Charlie, he has to be nice to everyone and meet all those old guys,' laughed Paddy.

Eoin and Paddy had captained their provinces in the interpro competition, but were delighted that Charlie had been given the much more difficult job of leading Ireland. It seemed to be one long round of shaking hands with men in blazers, and talking to TV reporters.

'The Welsh guys look like good crack,' said Sam. 'Will we go over and do a bit of mixing?'

'I suppose we'd better,' shrugged Eoin, who was some-times a bit nervous about meeting new people.

Paddy introduced himself to a group of players from each of the visiting teams, and welcomed them to Dublin.

'Not that I can welcome you to Dublin really,' he laughed. 'I'm from Enniskillen myself, it's up the coun-try.'

The other boys smiled, and began comparing notes on their places of origins and where they played rugby. They were all agreed that the sandwiches were excellent, but that there weren't enough of them.

One of the Scotland squad, Alistair Dods, had been on the team knocked out of the World Cup by a last-minute South African try. He admitted that he still woke up at night thinking about it.

'That was a terrible try to give away, and us with one foot in the semi-finals.' He shook his head. 'You guys took advantage of our bad luck though, and I was delighted that you ended up winning the whole thing.'

'Cheers!' said Eoin, 'that's very good of you to say that.'

'Maybe,' grinned Alistair. 'But we'll be well up for revenge when we play you on Saturday. We'll mince you.'

The other boys laughed, and Alistair smiled, but Eoin could see from his eyes that the defeat still hurt and the game against Scotland would likely be the toughest of the week.

Eoin rambled around, meeting up with boys he had played with and against in the European Cup and World Cup competitions. With the journalists' questions all answered and the men in blazers tucking into their drinks, Eoin sought out Charlie.

The Ireland captain looked a bit exhausted.

'Was training that hard today?' he asked.

'Not at all,' grinned Charlie. 'I was full of beans when I got in here. It's the shaking hands and smiling all the time that has tired me out!'

'Let's get out of here so,' suggested Eoin. 'Are you up for a stroll down to the stadium? Paddy was keen to see what it looks like at night.'

'That would be great,' said Charlie, 'I'll just check with Neil that my duties are over for the day.'

As Eoin strolled out to the lobby he bumped into Mr Carey, who had just arrived and seemed a bit flustered.

'Am I too late for the speeches?' he asked.

'Yes… about an hour late,' Eoin replied.

'Oh, I'd better get in and apologise to Neil. We were held up because we had to have a meeting after the game to organise the replay. Dodder Woods were trying to rush it next week, but we managed to delay it till after this thing is over.'

Eoin was puzzled. 'Replay?'

'Yes, of course it's a replay,' snapped Mr Carey. 'Haven't you heard the result? We drew 10-10 with Dodder in the semi-final.'

CHAPTER 19

It wasn't very far down to the Aviva stadium, but to Eoin and Charlie it felt like a simple skip and a jump as they discussed what might have happened to Castlerock.

'That's a low-scoring game,' said Charlie. 'Did you hear from Alan what went on?'

Eoin realised his phone had been switched off all day. He powered it up and waited for the messages to arrive.

'It sounds like Mr Carey made sure the replay was organised for after the tournament is over, which is good news for us,' grinned Eoin.

His phone buzzed seven or eight times.

'Alan,' he laughed. 'He was giving me updates after every score.'

Eoin sifted through the texts before finally getting a picture of what had gone on.

'The weather was brutal, it seems, and it was impossible to kick. The result was actually two tries each, so nobody kicked a conversion, even from under the posts. Richie Duffy had a chance to win it from right in front near the end, but the ball bounced twice before it rolled along the ground and settled beside the upright.'

'That's shocking,' said Paddy. 'I bet they'll be delighted to get you back.'

'Maybe,' grinned Eoin. 'Our pal Dylan scored the two tries so he'll think he can still do it on his own.'

They crossed the railway tracks and looked up at the stadium wall towering above with an eerie green glow.

'Wow, it looks huge from here. I've only been down once, for an Ulster game,' Paddy told them.

'Well Eoin certainly knows his way around this place – he's played here loads of times,' laughed Charlie.

'And you too,' said Eoin. 'Sure, the first time I was playing *against* you in the Father Geoghegan Cup final.'

'There's no need to bring that up,' grinned Charlie, 'Your jammy kick in garbage time…'

Eoin laughed and led them down to the gap between the stadium and the club house and souvenir shop.

'If we duck in here there's a gate we can climb over into the grandstand,' he whispered. 'There's a security guard in the box there so we'll have to make sure he doesn't see us.'

The guard was reading a newspaper but glanced up every few seconds to check the bank of screens that showed CCTV images of all parts of the stadium.

'We'll have to be very careful. If we're caught in here the IRFU might get very grumpy,' said Paddy.

Charlie paused, turning a little pale. 'You're right Paddy. And I'm the captain so they'll get even grumpier with me.'

He kicked a stone and thought for a moment. 'I think we'd better head back,' he said.

Eoin shrugged. 'Sure, what have we got to lose if we ask nicely?' He walked straight over to the security hut. 'Good evening sir, we're playing for Ireland here next week in the Under 16 Four Nations,' he said, pointing at the embroidered message on his jumper. 'Would you mind if we just walked down this tunnel to have a look inside the stadium? Paddy here has never seen it with the lights on.'

The security man looked them up and down and examined the jumpers closely.

'Under 16 you say,' he grumbled. 'Shouldn't you be in bed by now?' But he waved them down the slope towards the pitch. 'Don't touch anything and make sure you're back here in two minutes.'

Eoin thanked the man and they hurried away.

Paddy was open mouthed as the tunnel opened up to show the huge fifty-thousand-seater stadium with its glass walls and giant screens. He asked about the strange array of metal frames on wheels covering the pitch and Eoin explained that the special lights that hung from them were there to help the grass grow faster.

'I'm gonna close my eyes and see if I can imagine any of the great games that have taken place here,' said Paddy.

'As long as you don't imagine the Father Geoghegan Cup final,' laughed Charlie. 'That keeps coming up in my nightmares.'

Eoin's eyes swept across the field, and he took a little jump as he saw, walking across the field in the far corner, a single figure wearing a black, red, and yellow hooped jersey.

CHAPTER 20

oin was so relieved to see Brian that he started to walk towards the playing area before Charlie called him back.

'You can't go out there... see the sign?' he pointed out.

Eoin stopped. 'Yeah, sorry, you're right.' He looked over to where Brian was now bending over, digging at the pitch. He realised Charlie and Paddy knew nothing of Brian and the other ghosts that occasionally came into his life, and letting them in on it now would just make things too complicated.

The boys wandered back up the slope, Eoin checking on Brian a couple of times before he went out of sight. He wondered what his friend was doing and thought about sneaking out of the hotel later, but immediately decided against it.

'Just think, we'll be out there in a few days, wearing a green shirt. That will be some day,' grinned Paddy.

'If selected,' snickered Charlie. 'Which reminds me, Neil wants me to sit in on the selection chat tonight...'

he checked his watch. '… in two minutes.'

The captain took off like a frightened rabbit, scampering into the distance as his team-mates broke into laughter behind him.

Paddy and Eoin strolled back to the hotel, grateful again that Charlie had taken over the leadership duties.

They debated the selections they expected to see, with the main disagreement coming about scrum-half, where Eoin wanted Rory and Paddy went for Sam Rainey. Eoin didn't mention what Neil had told Mr Carey – that the Castlerock three were already pencilled in as first choices.

There were no real surprises when the team was released later that evening, with Rory retaining the scrum-half berth, and Roger Savage coming back to partner his brother in the second row after recovering from concussion. David Bourke, who played in the World Cup final, was injured and Dan Boyd from Enniskillen came in. 'They probably picked Dan so they won't have to change the initials on the gear,' joked Paddy.

Eoin read the team out to Paddy. 'Matthew Peak, Kuba Nowak, you, Dan, Ollie McGrath, me, Rory, Ultan Nolan, James Brady, John Young, the Savages,

Oisin Deegan, Charlie Bermo and Noah Steenson.'

'That's a decent team, we've a good chance in this,' Paddy chuckled.

'Maybe, but I think those Scots lads are really up for this game.'

Eoin was right. The defeat in the World Cup had really rankled with the Scottish boys, and they played like men possessed. It was a cold, windy day with driving rain and no chance of free-flowing rugby. Eoin even had to clap his hands together every couple of minutes to keep them warm.

Kicking was difficult too, and at half-time the scoreboard showed the evidence: Ireland led 3-0 thanks to the only simple kick of the half from straight in front of the goal, although the ball swung so much in the wind that it hit the inside of the post on its way over the bar.

'This is impossible,' grumped Rory at half-time. 'Even getting the ball five metres to Eoin without the wind taking it is tricky.'

'I know, I know,' said Neil, 'And you've all done very well so far. Just keep it tight and don't try anything fancy. We have a more powerful scrum and if we can keep the ball solid up front we'll get there.

But as the second half started the rain got heavier and the ground churned up so much that it became harder and harder to run through the mud.

'Let's just try to drive them up the middle,' suggested Charlie in a huddle with Eoin and Rory. 'It's tougher to go backwards in this muck and hopefully they'll give us a few penalties within kicking distance.'

It was grim rugby. Ireland won ruck after ruck, taking no chances and driving forwards inches at a time. Charlie always took the scrum option for penalties until, when a Scottish forward was caught offside with just five minutes left on the clock, the Ireland captain looked at Eoin, who replied with a nod.

'You'd kick this nineteen times out of twenty on a good day,' Charlie grinned, 'but that wind is ridiculous. Do you reckon you'll do it?'

Eoin winced. It was blowing a gale now, but he had practised for just this situation over the Christmas holidays. A wild storm had blown up one morning and he knew he needed to practise his kicking in such conditions. His mother had to defrost him in front of the fire when he got home.

Eoin grinned as he remembered that day, and paced out his run-up. He turned and faced the posts, tossing in the air the few blades of grass he could find that hadn't been drowned in mud. Although he was standing in midfield in front of the goal the wind took the grass and blew it over the heads of the spectators on the touchlines.

He exhaled and turned to stare at the posts before starting his run. He aimed far to the right of the right-hand post, a full cross-bar's width away. The ball swerved right before the wind caught hold of it and whipped it back the other way, dropping all the time before it fell, just inside the left-hand post and a metre over the bar.

The touch-judges looked at each other and raised their flags and a huge roar erupted as the Irish team leapt in the air.

The Scottish boys looked devastated, but Alistair Dods gathered them around and pointed at the clock. 'One last push,' he roared.

CHAPTER 21

The clock showed that there was less than two minutes left to play and Eoin focused on trying to burn off as much time as possible. As the rain bucketed down Ireland controlled the ball from the ruck and were preparing to run down the clock when Oisín made a fatal error.

The flanker slipped trying to stay attached to the ruck, and as he fell he turned and tried to pass the ball to Rory. The scrum-half was caught in the mud and just couldn't switch legs to take the ball cleanly.

A Scottish boot came powering through and kicked the ball down the field. What happened next became a much-watched video on YouTube for weeks after.

The Scottish backs set off in pursuit of the ball, and had a head-start on the Irish players who found themselves on the backfoot, struggling to get out of the mud. It looked just like a slow bicycle race, with the thirty players all trying to charge towards the ball, but none getting up above a fast walking pace.

Eoin could hear the laughing start in the crowd, and

got annoyed. But he was trying too hard to get moving to worry too much about it.

The Scottish No. 8 stretched his long legs faster than anyone else and was first to the ball just on the Irish 22 metre line. He picked it up and tried to run again, but had lost momentum in doing so. Ollie McGrath came charging across from the wing and tried to dive to make the tackle, but his feet refused to leave the ground and he just fell flat on his face into a puddle.

The laughter grew louder but the players were too focused to notice. Alistair was the next Scotsman to the ball and after he gathered he put his head down and tried to get moving but the Irish defence moved across, forcing him to take his 'run' wider and wider as they got nearer and nearer.

Eoin had given up the chase, realising it was hopeless from where he was on the field, but he roared his players on as the centres closed in on the Scottish captain. Squelch, slurp and splash were the only other sounds that could be heard as he neared the line, but on he plodded, now down to taking one desperate step at a time as the quicksand mud sucked him down.

He reached the line close to the corner flag, and was trying to cut back towards the post when a green blur flew through the air and knocked him flying. It was

Kuba, the speedy Connacht wing, and he managed to bring Alistair down just short of the line.

But as the referee struggled to catch up with the action, he – and everyone else on the ground – had no trouble seeing what happened next. A big hand, poking out of a dark blue sleeve, lifted the ball in the air and plunged it down just beside the flag.

'Prrrrrreeeep!' went the whistle, as the referee raised his arm aloft.

Eoin fell to his knees, as did most of the other boys. Some found it hard to get up again, and the replacements had to help the players extract themselves from the mud.

'That's 6-5,' muttered Charlie, 'Do you think he could kick that?'

Eoin shrugged. 'I wouldn't fancy it myself, but who knows.'

'Time's up anyway,' said Rory, pointing to the clock.

The ground was deathly silent as the Scottish boy lined up the kick. He was out wide on the left, two feet in from touch and with the ball teed up in the middle of a sea of mud, like a white cherry on a chocolate cake.

Inside, Eoin was willing him to miss of course, but he

also felt sorry for the kicker. Unable to run, he walked up to the ball and swung his boot back as far as it would go, driving the ball as hard as he could. It was a great effort, but without momentum he had no chance. The ball swung into the air but fell seven or eight metres short without ever getting up as high as the crossbar.

The crowd broke into cheers and the teams shook hands. Alistair Dods grimaced as he shook Paddy's hand and he commiserated with him.

'Och, sure it was a bit of a farce at the end but you were the better side,' Alistair told him.

'It was a shame it ended like that,' said Eoin. 'On a good day that would have been a really good game.'

CHAPTER 22

The Ireland dressing room was a joyful place, although it was almost impossible to see the expressions on the boys' faces. Neil suggested they all take a shower with their gear on first, to wash away most of the mud.

'That was a great display in one of the worst conditions for a rugby match I've ever seen,' the coach began. 'I'm sure, if it hadn't been such a short tournament with teams from overseas, that the ref would have abandoned it early. But full marks for sticking with it and getting the points.'

One of the coaches told them that because of the conditions the Wales v England game had been switched to the artificial grass pitch at the back of Aviva Stadium and the bus would drop off anyone that wanted to watch that game.

Eoin, Charlie, Paddy and Noah put up their hands and so, washed and changed and wrapped up warm, twenty minutes later they were standing on the touch-line watching thirty boys in red and white trying to battle with the same wind and rain – although they were spared the squelching mud.

After about ten minutes Charlie and Noah announced they had had enough.

'This is pointless,' Charlie said. 'You can't learn anything about the other teams in these conditions. Neil and the coaches are here and they'll bring us anything they've learned. I'm going back to the hotel for another hot shower.'

The pair jogged off, leaving Eoin and Paddy huddled under the back of the grandstand trying to keep the rain out of their faces.

They took note of the players who were the line-out targets, and which foot the half-backs kicked with, but by half-time they concluded that Charlie and Noah were probably right. The Welsh side seemed very weak and England were already fifteen points ahead.

'Do you want to head back so?' Eoin asked.

'I suppose,' Paddy replied, 'but can we go around the back there? I'd like to see a bit more of the stadium.'

The pair ambled off towards the northern end of the ground, ducking into a tunnel that led to the main pitch.

They sat down in a row of seats that were sheltered from the rain, and Eoin pointed out a few of the sights to Paddy, including the spot from where he'd kicked the penalty to win the Fr Geoghegan Cup way back in first year. He remembered that moment often, and how Brian had helped him get over his nervousness at being watched by twenty-five thousand people.

Just thinking about Brian was enough to make him look closely around the ground. He was worried that Brian hadn't been in touch for months, and the other ghosts weren't much help in finding him either. He was frustrated, too, that he hadn't been able to talk to him that evening in the stadium because he was with Paddy and Charlie.

'There's a lad over there in a rugby jersey,' said Paddy. 'I wonder is he going training. He didn't pick the best day for it, did he?'

Eoin looked across to the players' tunnel where Paddy was pointing. Just inside it stood Brian, who was staring across at them.

'Can you see him?' asked Eoin.

'Of course I can see him, it's not that far away,' replied Paddy.

'But…' Eoin trailed away. He had been able to see ghosts for several years now, but his friends could only see them when he brought them along and introduced them.

He lifted his arm to salute Brian, who saluted back and walked around the side of the field towards him.

'Do you know that guy?' asked Paddy.

Eoin said yes, but he wasn't sure whether to let his friend in on the whole story.

'He's called Brian, and that's a Lansdowne shirt. They're one of the clubs that plays here,' he told Paddy as the ghost made his way along the dead-ball line.

He introduced the pair and Paddy noticed how cold Brian's hand was – even for a day like they were having.

Brian looked worried, and after they had swapped small talk about rugby and the weather, Eoin told him about the tournament, and how he would likely be playing for Ireland in the final, probably deciding, game in the stadium, six days from now.

Brian looked even more worried then, and signalled to Eoin that he needed to talk to him.

'It's OK, Brian,' he said. 'Paddy's a good friend of mine, I'll explain to him about you later. What's up?'

'Well…' started Brian, 'I can't really be sure, but there are a lot of strange things happening around the stadium. Water keeps springing up from nowhere, and even before this rain today the pitch has been getting soaked. The groundsmen are doing their best on it, but it's almost like they're trying to turn back the tide.'

CHAPTER 23

Eoin frowned. 'I saw you here last night, you were out on the field there. Was that what you were doing?'

'Yes,' replied Brian. 'I've checked the particular corner every day and it never seems to dry out, even if there's weeks without rain – which doesn't happen too often in Dublin. I'm not even sure what can be done, but I've been getting a bad feeling about it and I'm not usually wrong.'

Eoin explained how he had met the four ghosts out in Castlerock – or 'Dave, Kevin, Alex and Will' as he called them to keep Paddy in the dark for the moment – and that they too had suspected something was up.

'They're keen to get in touch with you, Brian, can you drop out to see them? I won't be in school for another week.'

Brian nodded and said goodbye.

'But do drop back, Eoin, you might be able to help me with a few things,' he called, as the boys began their jog back to the hotel.

On the way, Paddy stopped.

'Who was your man?' he asked.

'Just Brian, an old guy who used to play for Lansdowne,' replied Eoin.

'So you said, but there's something a bit weird about him. That shirt for starters – it's like something your grandad would have worn. And what was he doing hanging around the stadium in the rain. He doesn't work there, does he?'

Eoin paused, and looked at Paddy before looking down at the ground. He had let a couple of his Castlerock friends in on the secret, and it was best if he didn't tell Paddy any lies.

'OK, but this might be a bit of a shock to you. And don't tell me I'm mad either… but… Brian is a ghost. A dead person's spirit. He was killed playing rugby in there,' he pointed back to the stadium.

Paddy nodded.

'Is that all?' he asked. 'Sure, I've seen loads of ghosts. My grandad lives in an old house over in Donegal and it's full of them. They're interesting characters too, not at all scary.'

Eoin laughed. 'I was afraid to tell you last night when we were here with Charlie. I've known Brian for a few years now. He's a great guy.'

'I must confess, none of my ghosts were rugby players,' replied Paddy. 'They were all farmers and fishermen.'

'Well, Brian wasn't the only one,' admitted Eoin. 'They all played rugby but one was also a soldier, another a student, as well as a prince and a priest.'

'How did you get to see them first?' asked Eoin.

'I'm not sure. It was grandad who first told me about them,' replied Paddy. 'He was very sick and we all went over to see him expecting him to die, but he got better. I was sitting with him one night and he told me the house was haunted, and would I like to see a ghost. I said "yes" and he whistled softly, and soon a couple of them arrived – a young woman and a little boy. They told me they'd died back in the Famine times.'

Eoin nodded, relieved that he was able share his secret with Paddy. 'I sometimes wonder why I was the first person ever to see Brian. I've never had to whistle for him either!"

CHAPTER 24

There was quite a buzz back at the hotel, with lots of parents and friends milling around the lobby talking to the Ireland players, who were buzzing after their win over Scotland.

Eoin spied Alan, who was sitting in the corner chatting to Charlie and Rory.

'Hey Al, great to see you. Did you bring us in the homework or what?' laughed Eoin.

Alan grinned back. 'Nah, I met Neil after the game and showed him the stats I'd compiled on the match. He asked me to come back here to give him a proper briefing.'

'Wow, that's really cool,' said Paddy. 'I hope you can prove I'm the best out-half in the squad?' he added with a grin.

'I don't think Stephen Hawking could prove that,' laughed Charlie.

The boys settled down to discuss the game further, and Eoin filled them in about the first-half of England's game against Wales.

'I'd say Neil will rest a few guys against Wales as they look fairly weak,' said Paddy.

'Maybe,' replied Charlie. 'But we can't afford to mess up like Leinster did in the interpros,' he grinned. The province had given all its top players a game off and been beaten by tournament dark horses Connacht.

Neil had indeed learned that lesson, although the reserve strength in the Ireland side was much greater than Ted had to work with at Leinster. He picked Sam Rainey ahead of Rory, and switched Eoin and Paddy so the Ulster half-back unit was intact. Eoin was happy enough, as he knew Paddy was a good player and he had enjoyed playing in the centre earlier in his career. It also meant he was matched up alongside another pal, Killian Nicholson from St Osgur's.

That was the extent of Neil's tinkering with the side, and the changes pepped them up against Wales. By half-time Ireland were 19-0 up and the second half turned into a rout. Eoin nipped in for a couple of tries and kicked twenty points as Ireland ran out 45-5 winners.

'Hey Eoin, you're a shoo-in for the golden boot,' laughed Alan as he joined the players on the field after the game. Alan was wearing a green tracksuit and hoodie and carried an IRFU clipboard – Neil had made him the official team stats man for the tournament and he couldn't have been happier.

'I've worked out the table after two games,' he told Charlie, handing him a scruffy piece of paper.

	Played	Won	Lost	Tries	Diff.	Points
Ireland	2	2	0	5	+41	8
England	2	2	0	9	+40	8
Scotland	2	0	2	3	-11	0
Wales	2	0	2	3	-70	0

'You have to feel sorry for the Scots lads,' said Eoin. 'Two really narrow defeats. But it's all down to this big game in the Aviva on Friday.'

'How do they decide who wins if that's a draw,' asked Charlie. 'We're one point ahead on points difference.'

'I checked,' replied Alan. 'And unfortunately, tries scored is what counts. So you'll just have to go out and win it.'

CHAPTER 25

The countdown to the deciding game began next morning with a team meeting in the hotel. Neil told them that there was now a huge amount of media interest in the game – Ireland v England was always a big game, no matter the sport – and the TV cameras would be there on Friday night too.

'Just remember you're representing your country, your school and your family when you're here. Don't do anything you wouldn't want the rest of the country to read about in the papers tomorrow....'

They spent the rest of the morning going through videos of England's first two games, with Neil frequently stopping the recording to point out the strengths or weaknesses he wanted his team to take note of.

'There's a big guy here called Ed Wood, he's enormous and a very good line jumper. We'll have to keep it away from him, or we'll be creamed in the line-outs. Their wings are sharp going forward, but not great tacklers and the right-wing looks a bit awkward when he has to turn and chase. Maybe dip some of your kicks in behind him early on Eoin, and Kuba, be ready for a sprint and chase.'

Neil told them he had lots of other insights, but would talk to them in smaller groups as he wanted them to focus on just a few 'learnings' as he called them.

Eoin took off after the meeting, keen to be on his own for a while, but also to return to the stadium. He was puzzled by what Brian was up to and keen to have a chat with him alone.

The clouds had cleared and it was a bright spring morning as he jogged down Lansdowne Road. He passed two boys wearing school uniforms that weren't from Castlerock, so he was astonished to hear them say 'That's your man Eoin Madden.' His mum had told him the night before that he had been mentioned on the local radio news after the win over Wales. Perhaps Neil was right – and this huge media interest would find its way down to little old Eoin.

He crossed the railway tracks and ran past the stadium to the back pitch where he had watched the game with Paddy. He vaulted the fence and did a few stretches before setting off to jog around the field. He reckoned that if he appeared to be a player doing some extra training he had less chance of being thrown out than if he started snooping around the stadium.

He cast his eyes around the ground as he ran, checking the entrances and stairwells for any sight of Brian. He skirted the field, jogging back beside the touchline that ran alongside the river. As he reached the corner and turned for home, his ankle went from under him and he fell against the fence. He was astonished to see his boot throw up a huge spray of water as he skidded across the artificial grass.

'Oof, that hurts,' he muttered, as he sat on the ground massaging his ankle. 'Nothing broken though.'

He examined the ground where he sat, pushing down into the soil and finding that water squelched up every time he did so.

'I thought this stuff was all-weather and drained really quickly,' he mused. 'It stopped raining about eight o'clock last night so that's pretty slow going.'

Eoin got himself gingerly to his feet and limped off back towards the hotel. He decided to take his time as he didn't want any awkward questions from Neil and the inevitable trip to the physio, and maybe even doubts over whether he could play against England. He didn't want to take any chances with that, so when he neared the railway crossing and noticed that a train was coming he made the quick decision that he needed to visit his old pals in Castlerock.

CHAPTER 26

Wednesday was a half-day in Castlerock, and Eoin arrived just as the classes were breaking up. The first-years were excited to see their international star player and he had to politely turn down a couple of requests for selfies.

'I'm in a hurry, sorry,' he said as he took the steps of the school two at a time.

Inside, he bumped into Mr McCaffrey. 'Eoin. Is everything all right? I thought you'd be in town with the Ireland team? Congratulations on how you've been doing, by the way.'

'Thank you, sir,' replied Eoin. 'We just had the afternoon off and I wanted to collect a book so I can keep up with my reading,' he said. That was the first time Eoin had even thought of study, but he reckoned Mr McCafferty would be impressed.

'Very good, very good,' replied the headmaster. 'Now run along, I've got to see how the Junior Cup team are doing in your absence. I trust you'll be back for the replay?'

'I think so sir,' replied Eoin. 'When is it?'

'Next Saturday morning,' he answered.

Eoin gasped. 'But our last game is Friday night…'

'Really? Oh dear, that's not ideal,' frowned the head-master. 'Oh well, perhaps you could take it easy against England, and maybe ask the coach to take you off at half-time. Actually, I'll get Mr Carey to ask him.'

Eoin looked closely at Mr McCafferty's face, trying to work out if he was joking, but couldn't see even a single wrinkle or quiver around his mouth. But surely he wouldn't want Eoin – and Ireland – to miss out on a chance of winning the Triple Crown?

Eoin said goodbye and started up the stairs to his dormitory room. Mentioning the book had unleashed a twinge of guilt that he was missing a whole week of study with his Junior Cert exams just over the horizon.

He tried the doorknob, and was surprised to see it open, and delighted to see that Alan was there at the desk, scribbling away.

'Hey, Eoin, what has you back here? Are they going for Joe Kelly for the last game?' grinned Alan.

'No chance,' smiled Eoin, sitting down on his bed. 'I just took a last-minute decision to come out to say hello. I twisted my ankle and wanted to walk it off in case Neil got grumpy.'

'Speaking of grumpy, Dylan has just been here. He's heard the replay is the day after the final and now he's not sure if he wants you, Charlie and Rory in the team. I told him not to be stupid and he stormed off.'

Eoin laughed. 'Thanks for the support Al, but I'm not sure I would have put it quite that way.'

'How are you getting on?' he asked, nodding at the pile of text books and copy books on the desk.

'Not bad,' Alan replied. 'I missed a couple of days with the matches so I'm trying to catch up.'

'Me too,' said Eoin. 'I'm happy enough with the study, but I need to reread one of the novels.'

He reached up to the shelf above his bed and pulled out the book he was looking for, but as he did so another book came loose and fell on to his bed.

'What's that?' asked Alan.

'It's the book about Lansdowne Road that Grandad gave me for Christmas,' Eoin replied.

He picked up the book and went to hand it to Alan when his friend suddenly jumped, pointing over Eoin's shoulder. Eoin turned and was confronted by Brian, looking even more worried than he had the last time they met.

'Eoin,' started Brian. 'How on earth did I get here?'

'I don't know,' Eoin replied. 'I just picked up this

book… it's about the history of the rugby ground.'

'I was just over in Lansdowne,' said the ghost, 'I was wandering around and checking on all the weird things that are happening there when suddenly I arrived here.'

'Maybe it's the book?' suggested Alan. 'Remember when it was the Dave Gallaher book that first summoned his ghost…'

Eoin flicked through the pages. 'I wonder…'

'What sort of weird things are happening, Brian?' asked Alan.

'There's been a lot of puddles forming in the basement where all the motor cars are, and the pitch is a lot wetter than it should be,' replied Brian. 'But the really weird stuff happened today when I saw dozens of creatures just fleeing from the grounds – mice, rats, even a family of foxes. They were making for the river bank. It's as if they know there's something wrong.'

Eoin checked his watch and put the two books into a plastic bag. 'I have to dash to catch the train back. I'll read through the book again tonight and see if I can come up with anything.'

CHAPTER 27

ack in the hotel lobby, Eoin bumped into Charlie.

'Hey skipper, what's happening?' he grinned.

'Oh, the usual headaches,' sighed Charlie as he settled down into an armchair. 'Roger Savage has to do a fitness test, and the IRFU media man is never off the phone setting up interviews with me. I must have done fifteen with the newspapers and websites already, and three or four for the radio. The media guy gives you pointers on what you can and can't say – so it's easy enough – but it's very tiring still.'

Eoin laughed. 'When are the TV guys coming? Myself and Paddy can bounce around behind you making bunny ears.'

'Don't you dare,' said Charlie. 'They're meeting me down in the stadium first thing in the morning so steer clear of that, please. There's four stations want to interview me. If I knew this was part of the job I'd have turned it down.'

The boys joined the rest of the team for their evening meal, before Charlie had to join the coaches for a selection meeting. The team had been remarkably lucky to get through the first two games without any serious injury and all the names were in the hat for the decider.

Eoin wandered up to the room he was sharing with Killian, who was already snoring loudly. He watched TV for a few minutes before he remembered the Lansdowne book and fetched it from his bag.

He riffled through the pages and read Brian's story again, before starting at the opening chapter. He read about how the original ground had been laid out on a land that was virtually a swamp, and was amazed that they used to keep a flock of sheep to keep the grass short in those days before grass-mowers were invented. He laughed at the story of how the original owner, Henry Dunlop, had to row out to the middle of the field to collect the sheep that had become stranded by flood waters.

He wondered if it had any connection with the marshy ground in which he had twisted his ankle, but before he had any more time to think about it, the book fell from his hand and he nodded off to sleep.

Eoin didn't return to the book until the morning of match-day. He woke early and looked across to the other bed where Killian was still asleep There was no point getting up too soon as the match wasn't until five o'clock and the only squad activity planned was a fifteen-minute run around on the pitch around lunchtime.

He picked the book up from the floor and began to read. It was fascinating to learn how the ground had been selected by Mr Dunlop, and drained to allow him to lay down a cinder running track. He was a small, whiskered man who spent most of his life building up the ground so it could host lots of sporting events, like croquet, archery, tennis, cricket and cycling, but by the time of his death it was solely used for rugby.

Eoin examined the old maps that showed the area before the ground was built, and saw there was a distillery on the site where they made whiskey. He turned the page on its side, and upside down, to get his bearings, and found the River Dodder. He looked closely at the map and was puzzled by what he saw, but the writing was too small so he decided to ask Alan later if he could make sense of it. He slipped the book into his match-day bag and started to pack for the big day ahead.

CHAPTER 28

It was a sunny morning, so after breakfast Eoin and Paddy went for a walk around the leafy suburb in which their hotel was situated. They passed groups of boys and girls walking to school and almost every one of them pointed them out or called 'good luck' after them. Even the occasional motorist beeped their horn at the pair. Eoin hated the attention, but Paddy was delighted.

'We're celebrities now,' he chuckled. 'They'll make me Lord Mayor of Enniskillen when I get home, I reckon.'

'Yeah, I get an awful lot of banter when I go home to Ormondstown. I'm not sure they would want me to be Lord Mayor though.' Eoin's home town was in Munster, which had made it awkward when he had his break-through success with Leinster.

They found a park and sat and watched the world go by for an hour, chatting about almost everything *except* rugby. Eoin liked that, he preferred to block out an upcoming game, especially the big ones. It wasn't that he suffered particularly from nerves, just that he liked to go into a game with a clear mind and with just a couple of his coach's instructions to focus upon.

They hired a pair of tennis rackets and bashed a ball about for a while before they realised they needed to be back at the hotel and ready to leave for the ground in half an hour.

As they jogged back they were surprised to bump into Charlie, leaning over a garden wall and looking glum.

'What's up Charlie, we're leaving for the ground shortly?' Paddy asked.

'Ah I just needed to get out of the hotel and all the match talk,' Charlie replied. 'And I got a call from Mr McCaffrey telling me to take myself off at half-time...'

'Me too,' said Eoin. 'He told me to tell Neil. I'm not going to, are you?'

'I did already,' sighed Charlie. 'He laughed at first, then blew his top. Then he threatened to take the captaincy off me.'

'He wouldn't dare,' Eoin frowned. 'This is none of your doing. I wish these adults could sort themselves out instead of leaving it to us. It's very unfair.'

Charlie smiled sheepishly.

'OK, well let's get down there and see what we can do.'

Back at the hotel, the trio brought their bags down to the lobby and waited to load them onto the bus. Neil signalled to Charlie that he wanted to speak to him, but Eoin nipped in ahead of him to buttonhole the coach.

'Neil, I'm sorry,' he started, 'but I'm in the same boat as Charlie – and probably Rory too. Our headmaster is insisting that you take us off at half-time. Now, I don't mind if you leave me on – I can take the heat – but Charlie's really stressed by it. Can you have a word with Mr Carey?'

Neil nodded. 'This sort of interference is unbeliev-able, and the last thing I need on a match day like this. I'll ring him and see if he can call off the hounds.'

Neil left the lobby and Eoin turned back to his pals.

'He's going to call Carey – hopefully *he* can make McCaffrey see sense.'

CHAPTER 29

With three games due to be played on the main stadium pitch that day, time was tight and rigidly controlled down at the Aviva. The Ireland squad was allocated fifteen minutes to get used to the feel of the turf under the feet and to work out the pitch dimensions and angles. Eoin had played there several times before but he never lost the sense of excitement – or the feeling that it was a great honour to play there.

Afterwards, Neil talked to them in the dressing room and suggested they go back to the hotel for a light lunch and then either rest or come down and watch the Wales v Scotland game.

Strolling back with Noah and Paddy, Eoin checked his phone and noticed that he had got a text from Alan.

'r u gonna watch Wal v Sco game?'

He texted back.

'Yes. Meet you in front of stand at 2.15.'

'That's Alan,' he told his friends, 'he must have bunked off for the afternoon.'

The boys laughed. 'I hope he's wearing a disguise 'cos

all the games are being shown live on the TV,' chuckled
Noah.

As they reached the hotel he was delighted to see a
familiar car in the carpark with Tipperary registration
plates, but he still pretended to be surprised when his
mum and dad sprang out on him in the lobby.

'Thanks for coming, Mam,' he said, 'is Dixie here too?'

'I am indeed, and thank you for enquiring,' came a
voice from behind a giant potted plant. Out stepped
his grandfather, wearing a bright green bobble hat on
his head.

'Do you like my supporters' gear?' he asked. 'Your
mother wouldn't allow me to wear a replica shirt. She
said it was undignified for a man my age.'

'I'm sure you would look fine,' laughed Eoin. 'Are
you staying for lunch?'

'We've just had some,' explained his dad, 'but we'll
come in and look at you eating if you like. We're going
to scoot off to do some shopping for a while but we'll
be down at the ground for five o'clock.'

Eoin was very happy to escape from the rest of the
team and their pre-match talk, and enjoyed hearing all
the news from home from his parents and Dixie. They

told him how the gang of bicycle thieves had been rounded up and all their friends had got their bikes back.

'I'll get home for a couple of days over Easter,' Eoin told them, 'but I'd say that will be my only trip home until the summer exams are over.'

When lunch was over, Eoin organised that his family got some complimentary tickets to sit in the president's box and told them he'd give them a wave at some stage before the game. He picked up his bag and strolled back down to the stadium alone.

Alan was sitting in the front row of the West Stand, but as soon as Eoin mentioned the live television coverage he turned white and pulled his green bobble hat down over his face.

'Let's get out of here,' he snapped. 'I'm supposed to be in school till half-past three.'

Eoin laughed and the pair relocated to the back row of the stand, where they sat behind a large crowd of Scottish supporters.

They chatted about the game, and Alan filled him in on a few stats that he thought Eoin should know such as the number of times the England out-half passed, ran or kicked the ball. He took his stats-man kit out of his bag

– pencils, pens, notebooks, calculators, old programmes and a huge magnifying glass.

Eoin laughed. 'What's that for?'

Alan blushed. 'I need a pair of binoculars, but I can't afford them. This was the next best thing I could find lying around at home.'

'But it makes you look ridiculous, like some sort of Sherlock Holmes…'

Eoin stopped, and checked his own bag.

'Actually, that's just the thing – I have a job for that,' he said. 'There's a map here with very small print that I'd like you to take a look at.'

Eoin opened the page and explained to Alan that it was a two hundred and fifty-year-old map of the site of what later became the stadium in which they were now sitting. He drew a box with his finger to show where the pitch now was. His friend peered closely through the magnifying glass and read…

'That line there says, "Primrose Stream" and that other one says "Mill Stream".'

Eoin stopped and pointed across the field where the Scots had just scored another try.

'So… behind that stand is the River Dodder, and down the back of that lower stand runs the River Swan. And there's two streams running underneath the stadium too.'

Eoin tucked the book back into his bag and sat back in his seat. His mind was racing, unsure what to do next.

'What's going on, Eoin?' asked Alan.

Eoin filled him in on what Brian had been up to and the strange happenings around the ground.

'No wonder there's water coming up everywhere – its built on a swamp!'

'You have to tell someone,' said Alan, 'but who? And not now, with a big match kicking off in an hour or so.'

'I'm still working that out,' agreed Eoin. 'I'll have to get the game out of the way first.'

Eoin checked the stadium clock and reckoned the Wales v Scotland game was ticking into its last minute or two. The result wouldn't have any effect on the competition, but both sets of players were still giving it everything they had.

'This is probably the last time most of these guys will wear their country's colours,' mused Alan. 'They're really going for it.'

'It will be the last time most of us wear it too,' replied Eoin. 'And it's such an honour. You just have to grab it with both hands and do everything you can for the team because there's no guarantee you'll ever get another chance. I'd love to come back here some day and play for Ireland in the Six Nations, but it will take a lot of work – and a good bit of luck too,' he added.

'Well my only hope of getting capped for Ireland is as a match analyst,' grinned Alan. 'I'll have to do maths in college I suppose.'

The referee's whistle sounded and the Scots boys raised their arms in the air after a hard-fought 22-16 win.

'I better go,' said Eoin, standing up quickly. 'I've got to talk to Neil about this McCaffrey thing too. Wish me luck.'

Eoin skipped down the steps two at a time before taking the lift down to the dressing room area deep in the grandstand. All the team were there already, and Neil tapped his wristwatch as Eoin trotted in.

'Sorry, Neil, I was watching the end of the Scottish match and just let the time slip away.'

'OK, but time is tight. Now sit down and listen while I make a few comments.'

Neil took the players through their main moves again, and highlighted a couple of England players who would need extra attention.

When he was finished, Eoin hurried into his kit, and as he tied up his bootlaces noticed Neil looming over him.

'Mr Carey won't answer his phone,' he snapped. 'And won't answer my texts either. So what do you propose I do?'

Eoin frowned. 'Leave this with me,' he replied. 'I'll be back in five minutes.'

'No, be back in three. We're on a strict schedule here.'

Eoin scampered out of the dressing room and pushed his way through to get out to the tunnel. The crowd in the grandstand started to clap, but when they saw he was on his own there was a mixture of laughter and jeers. Eoin ignored it and made a beeline for the president's box. He went over in his head what he was going to say, nervous that he would get tongue-tied and forget what he wanted to get across. He ignored the well-wishers and questioning from spectators, and headed straight for where the senior Castlerock teachers were sitting. He gestured to the headmaster and asked him to come to the back of the seated area.

'Sir, I'm sorry to disturb you, but I'm pretty busy myself and this is very important.' Eoin cleared his throat and began, 'I'm going to tell our coach that you *don't* want myself, Rory or Charlie to be taken off at half-time. I'm going to say you realise how important this game is for rugby followers in our country, and it would be unfair with so many people watching here, and at home on TV, to damage our chances of winning just to help one school. To play for Ireland is a rare honour, but so is playing for our school. You can be sure Rory, Charlie and I will be there tomorrow morning doing our very best for Castlerock College.'

Mr McCaffrey's mouth dropped open, and then closed once again. Eoin was terrified he was going to explode with fury, and have him dropped from the JCT, or maybe even expelled.

The headmaster stared at Eoin before speaking. 'I… I… I don't know what to say,' he started. 'But you're ab-so-lute-ly right,' he went on, emphasising each syllable. 'I'll talk to you later, but just go out there and do your very best for Ireland.'

Eoin grinned, nodded, and rushed off to join his team in the tunnel. He searched with his eyes and found Neil at the back of the group, so he flashed him a thumbs-up. The coach smiled back and returned the signal.

CHAPTER 30

The big crowd got behind Ireland, but it still wasn't enough to prevent England storming into an early 7-0 lead. Despite Neil's warnings, the giant second-row Ed Wood was unbeatable at the lineout, plucking the ball from the sky no matter who was throwing it and who they were aiming at.

The Irish forwards were in disarray and England took advantage, making ground through a series of rucks before finding their left winger who raced over in the corner and under the posts.

Charlie gathered his forwards together for a huddle and they appeared to come up with a plan as Eoin and Rory looked on. Charlie then took Eoin aside.

'Let's try to keep a lid on it for a while,' he suggested. 'There's no point kicking for touch with that lad winning everything. Let's bring the backs more into the game, and try the odd garryowen.'

Eoin nodded. He had pretty much decided that was how he needed to operate from now, so he was reassured that Charlie agreed.

As half-time approached and no more points had been scored, Eoin launched a huge kick high into the sky above the stadium. It hung in the air for half a second before it started its descent, by which time half a dozen green shirts were charging towards where they expected it to fall.

The England full-back stood under the ball but, fatally, glanced at the onrushing Irishmen. The momentary distraction ensured he missed the ball's flight and it bounced off his chest towards the attackers.

The referee signalled the knock-on, but allowed the advantage. Paddy scooped up the ball and once he hit his stride there was no catching him and he dived over just to the left of the posts.

Paddy was still grinning at half-time as the teams trotted up the tunnel with the scoreboard blinking '7-7' behind them.

'Great garryowen, Eoin,' he announced, slapping his pal on the back. 'You launch a few more of them in the second half and I'll be there to pick up the pieces.'

Eoin smiled and guzzled a bottle of water as he waited for Neil to have his say.

Charlie came over and sat beside him, and Eoin filled him and Rory in on what he said to Mr McCaffrey.

'Whaaaaaat?' he laughed. 'You've some tough neck

Eoin. And he even apologised to you? You really need to go into politics when you're finished school.'

'Ah, look, it needed to be said. We're fit enough to be able to cope with two games in twenty-four hours – or sixteen hours, even!'

'I hope you're right,' sniggered Rory, nursing a bruise that was starting to bloom on his forearm.

Neil was pleased at the way they had minimised the number of lineouts, and went through the plans for the second half. He reminded Eoin of his favourite chip-and-run into the corner move and suggested he attempt it early in the second half.

Eoin stood up and stretched before deciding at the last minute to use the loo in a room off the dressing-area. He washed his hands quickly, but just as he turned to exit the side-room he noticed a small, elderly man had appeared. He wore an old-fashioned suit with a shirt whose collar was pointed upwards, and his white hair sat on top of a heavily-bearded and whiskered face. He looked like Santa might, if he got an office job.

'Hello young man, and you are called Eoin Madden I believe,' the old man said.

Eoin nodded. 'How do you know my name?'

'Ah, I've seen a lot of you recently. My friend Brian Hanrahan has told me a great deal about you too.'

Eoin stared at the man, who he recognised from somewhere.

'Look, I've a big match to play and the second half is about to start, can we talk later?' he asked.

'Of course, run along,' replied the man.

'And who will I ask for? And where?' asked Eoin.

'Of course, well… everybody around here should know me – I built this place of course, although it *was* nearly one hundred and fifty years ago. Just ask for Henry Dunlop.'

CHAPTER 31

oin raced out to the playing field where his team were already getting into position for his kick-off. He looked around the stadium and was surprised to see people were coming in all the time and the lower levels were almost full.

His mind was racing as he considered the new ghost who had just entered his life. Why was his life so complicated? He shook his head, attempting to bring his thoughts into focus.

'Preeeeep' went the referee's whistle and Eoin carted the ball in the air for the forwards to scrap over. He had held the ball back a bit, knowing that an aerial contest would play into England's hands. After a series of rucks, Rory fired the ball back to Eoin, who had an extra half a second to play with and used it to measure his cross-field kick to perfection.

England's right-winger turned to chase but his momentum had been interrupted and he was slow to get going again. The English player just caught a blur of green as Kuba nipped in behind him and gathered the ball at speed. He was fifteen metres from the line and made no mistake in claiming the five points.

He had cut inside enough to give Eoin an easier chance to convert and he duly collected the extra two.

'This is fantastic,' grinned Rory as Eoin trotted back after the kick.

'Take it easy, Rors,' he replied. 'Seven points can go in the blink of an eye and they have some very dangerous players.'

'He's right,' said Charlie. 'We're getting battered in the line-outs and their scrum is very solid too. We're going to have to tackle everything that moves for the next twenty-five minutes.'

Charlie was proved correct, as England's superior physical strength ensured they dominated possession and territory for the rest of the game.

Ireland held out until there was just over six minutes left. England had used their line-out superiority to drive the ball down the field, and Ed Wood was their trump card every time. A line-out five metres from the Irish line was impossible to defend, and the white-shirted giant leapt high to collect the ball before falling side-ways over the line where he touched down.

That meant the conversion was tricky however, and the strong breeze that skirled and whistled around the

Aviva was hard to master. Eoin watched as the kicker tried to assess where the wind was coming from, and smiled inwardly as he hooked it well wide.

But the two-point margin was wafer thin and the crowd knew that it would take a superhuman effort by Ireland to defend it against such powerful opponents.

Play resumed and the green shirts battled hard to hold on to their lead, but England were finding gaps and making runs all the time and Ireland's defence grew weary at the unceasing attempts to break them down.

Eoin glanced up at the clock and saw just fifty seconds remained to play. He steeled himself for one last effort.

England controlled the ball at the base of the scrum, and inched forward. The scrum-half toyed with the ball, like a cobra choosing his moment to strike. He looked up, checked the position of his out-half, and fired it out to him. The No. 10 caught the ball, and swung back his boot, aiming for the corner where there would be time for one last line-out close to the Irish line.

But he never did get that kick away. As he swung, Noah came charging through and flung himself bravely at the No.10, who collapsed in a heap, the ball bobbling sideways off his foot along the ground.

Eoin, who had spotted what was going to happen

and had been following up, booted it forwards as hard as he could and set off in pursuit. With the England backs chasing him hard, he picked the ball up just outside their 22-metre line and heard an enormous roar from the crowd urging him onwards. On he ran, finally running out of steam just as he got to the line and fell over it, under the posts.

He barely had a chance to stand before he was floored once more, this time by fourteen boys in green who were overcome with delight. When they finally released him from the group hug, he looked up at the clock to see the game was over.

With a huge grin, he picked up the ball and ran back a few metres. He was about to take a drop-kick conversion like he had seen in a Sevens game on TV, but wasn't sure if that was legal and, anyway, he decided that he really wanted to enjoy the moment.

He placed the ball and looked up at the posts, remembering the first time he had taken a last-minute kick here. Sure enough, Brian appeared beside them this time too, and Eoin lifted his hand in salute.

But Brian wasn't smiling, and didn't call out any suggestion about where to aim for either.

'Come meet me as soon as you can after the game,' he shouted. 'I'll be down in this corner of the stand,' he said, pointing urgently to the north-east corner of the ground.

Eoin was a bit rattled by this, but kept his calm enough to slot the ball over the crossbar before once again he found himself at the bottom of a mound formed by his overjoyed team-mates.

CHAPTER 32

Eoin was walking off the field, waving to his family, when he was grabbed by a TV interviewer. She put a microphone in front of his face and demanded he tell the outside world just how it felt to win the Four Nations for Ireland.

Eoin shrugged, grinned and muttered a few words about how great a team he was part of and how the coach had done a great job, but ignored her request to explain what he was feeling.

And that was for a very good reason, because instead of 'delighted', 'thrilled' and 'overjoyed', Eoin's main emotions were 'distracted', 'confused' and 'terrified' as he struggled to work out why Brian wanted to see him so urgently.

He rejoined his team-mates and watched as Charlie went up to collect the trophy. He joined the queue for medals and waved again to Dixie and his parents while he collected his.

As the players made their way off the field, and the women's teams raced on, Eoin slipped away down the front of the stand and around to where Brian had pointed to minutes before.

He spotted his friend at the back of the empty lower level of the East stand, beckoning him to join him. Eoin raced up the steps, his boots making a racket, and was out of breath when he reached Brian.

'So… what's the urgency…?' he gasped.

'Come quickly,' Brian snapped, 'I need you to let people know what's been happening here, no one else can see or hear me.'

Eoin followed his friend out the doorway at the back of the stand, and stayed close behind as he descended a flight of steps.

'Look,' said Brian, pointing to a huge concrete pillar, his finger moving down to where it met the floor. Running up from the ground for about fifty centimetres was a crack wide enough for Eoin to insert his finger.

'That's a bit big for such a new stadium,' frowned Eoin.

'It's not the only one, I'm afraid,' answered Brian.

He brought him to see two other pillars that had similar cracks, and two panes of glass in the outer wall that were also fracturing so they looked like a giant spider's web. He then ushered him down under the north stand to a quiet area where the spare goalposts and corner flags were stored.

'Mind your footing here,' advised Brian, 'it gets very slippy.'

He led him in behind a large grass mower and pointed at the ground.

All Eoin could see in the gloom was a dark hole, but as he got nearer he heard gurgling and the sound of water rushing.

'It's a sinkhole – and down there is a river!' he cried. 'I saw an old map of this area and there are two rivers and two streams around here.'

'Yes,' replied Brian. 'And one of the old streams seems to have become full of water. With the building on the site it must have been buried, but now it's coming back and it looks like it's being causing this – and could cause a lot more trouble.'

'When did you discover this?' Eoin asked.

'Well, like I told you before, I saw some strange things happening around the stadium, with lots of water appearing where it shouldn't, and then this morning I noticed those cracks in the pillar and the…'

Brian stopped, noticing they had been joined by another person.

'This is Henry,' he told Eoin.

'I know, we met earlier,' Eoin replied as he nodded to

the gentleman whose idea it had been to build a sports ground on this site many years before.

'Henry has been around just in the last few days,' Brian explained.

'Indeed,' said Mr Dunlop. 'I found myself aroused from my slumber by an unshakeable dread that my life's work was under threat. I arrived here to find Brian and his friends hard at work searching for the root of the problem. It appears now he has found it,' he added, gazing at the hole in which the sound of the water rushing appeared to be growing louder.

'It was just before the game started today that I noticed it,' said Brian. 'I had been around here with Kevin Barry just two days ago and there was no sign of anything like this. You really cannot delay letting people know. Hurry, Eoin...'

Eoin swept his hair back from his brow and tried to gather his thoughts. He would probably have to answer some awkward questions on what he was doing down in this part of the ground, but he really needed to let the stadium authorities know about the sinkhole.

'Right, stay here and I'll be back as soon as I can convince someone I'm not raving mad.'

CHAPTER 33

Eoin raced as fast as he could around to the dressing rooms, where he met one of the IRFU officials who had presented the medals.

'Excuse me, sir, can I have a word?' he asked.

The man stared down at Eoin, looking puzzled.

'Sir, I was just over at the far corner of the ground,' he told him, pointing in the general direction of where he had met Brian and Henry. 'I wanted to warm down with a jog but the women were on the pitch...'

'Yes, yes, yes,' he said impatiently. 'Now, what's the problem?'

'So... Well... I noticed the glass panels in the wall were cracked, and when I looked at the pillars near them, they were cracked too. So, I went into the tunnel and, well, I found this huge sinkhole. The water....

The official's eyes bulged, and he stammered a reply.

'A sinkhole?... In the stadium?...Where...'

The man looked around from left to right, trying to find someone who could help. He spotted a policeman and called him over.

'Tell this garda what you told me while I go and find the manager. It's over in the north-east corner isn't it. We'll see you there.'

The garda grinned at Eoin – 'You were the lad who found the trophy before Christmas, weren't you?' he asked.

Eoin blushed, and remembered that the garda had given him some snacks when he was confined to the garda station before the raid on the thieves' hideout.

The garda chatted about that night as he led him around the service tunnel, but Eoin wasn't really listening because his mind was still focused on the pit.

'Here it is sir,' he gestured, and the garda switched his torch on to get a better view.

'Holy moley!' gasped the policeman. 'That's terrifying. Step back, son.'

The garda switched on his radio and asked to speak to his superior officer. He explained what he had seen just as a large group of IRFU and stadium officials arrived.

Eoin again showed them the evidence of the damage and it took just one brief look at the sinkhole for them to spring into action.

Two of the men raced off, bringing back crash barriers which they stretched across the tunnel so no one else could get past. Several other officials shouted into their mobile phones while the stadium manager stood and stared into the hole. He moved away and collared the garda – 'We'll have to evacuate the stadium immediately,' he said. 'We can't take any chances with this. The whole stand could collapse – and on live television.'

Eoin nodded and said he'd better go back to change out of his rugby kit in the dressing room.

'Yes, but hurry,' said the garda. 'And don't bother changing there. Just grab your bag and get out.'

As Eoin jogged back in front of the west stand he saw the fourth official wave the referee towards her and explain that the match would have to be abandoned.

There was much confusion among the players, who stood with their hands on their hips out in the field waiting to see what was happening. But when they heard the stadium announcer say, 'Please leave the ground via the nearest exit, the game has been abandoned and we must evacuate the stadium' they realised the seriousness of the matter.

Eoin slipped into the dressing room, where everything had been cleared out except his kit bag. He grabbed it, and took the hanger on which he had left his jacket and trousers and slung them over his shoulders.

As he made for the exit door he saw that someone had come into the room and was now sitting down on

141

one of the benches, his hands on his knees.

'Henry,' he gasped. 'Did you hear they're evacuating the stadium?'

'I did, I did,' he sighed. 'And I'm mightily saddened that they had to do such a thing. My poor old ground…

'Did you know when we built the first east stand over there, we got half the Irish Army to fill the upper deck to test its safety before they would let us admit paying customers. The men, in full uniform, had to jump up and down! But it all worked out for the best.'

Eoin suggested they leave, because the officials were concerned the new east stand might collapse – 'that could even have a domino effect around the ground' he told Henry.

'Yes, you must hurry away, but I will stay here. I spent much of my life around here, steadily improving the stadium and making it better and safer. If it's going to go, then I should go with it. Now leave!'

Eoin nodded, and gathered up his things again and ran. He was probably the last man out of the tunnels, and raced to catch up with the rest of his team who were standing a safe distance away.

'What kept you, Eoin?' snapped Neil.

'Sorry, Coach, I was the one that found the problem. I was showing it to the gardaí.'

'Oh, I didn't realise,' he replied. 'What exactly did you discover?'

Eoin recounted the story to an ever-growing audience. When he finished he got a clap on the back from Paddy.

'Fair play Eoin,' he grinned. 'And a little help from those ghosts too, no doubt?'

Eoin grimaced and shook his head, trying to make Paddy shut up.

'Ghosts?' asked Noah. 'What ghosts?'

'Sssshhh,' said Eoin. 'Paddy's only messing.'

Neil took Eoin aside.

'Eoin, did Paddy mention ghosts? Did you see one?'

Eoin didn't move, and kept his mouth closed.

'It's just that… well there have been rumours about ghosts around the stadium for a long time, but I've never heard of anyone meeting one,' said Neil. 'Will you tell me more, back in the hotel?'

Eoin nodded gently, and picked up his bag. He had just remembered his parents had been in the stadium and he wanted to make sure they – and Dixie – were safe.

CHAPTER 34

Eoin found Dixie, Mr Finn and his parents back in the hotel lobby, which was packed with people buzzing around and watching the dramatic happenings at the stadium on television.

'I was worried about you,' said his mother, 'I told Dixie you would surely be nosing around trying to find out what was going on. I'm glad you got out of that place – do you know what's happening?'

Eoin shrugged. If his mother knew that he had been right at the heart of the action she would be upset. He told them he thought it had been a problem with one of the grandstands and that the engineers were arriving just as he was leaving.

They chatted about the match for a few minutes but everyone was pre-occupied with the drama back at the stadium.

'I'm going up to lie down,' said his mum. 'This excitement is too much for me.' His parents left the table and Eoin stretched out his legs.

'So, what really happened, Eoin?' asked Dixie.

Eoin went red. 'What do you mean? I told you.'

'No, you told us some cock and bull story about a problem with the stands,' the old man smiled. 'And why did you get out of the stadium ten minutes after everyone else? Mr Finn here saw you come out.'

Eoin looked at the ground. 'Well… I didn't want to worry Mam…'

'That's fine,' said Dixie. 'She does get into a panic about you whenever you're tackled, so you're right to keep anything worrying from her. But what actually did happen?'

Eoin shrugged again. 'Well… I went for a run around the back of the stands and I saw some cracks, and then I found a huge hole in the ground with a river running through it. I got one of the IRFU guys and a garda to take a look, and then I scarpered.'

Dixie looked closely at Eoin.

'Well,' he said. 'That might have frightened your mother right enough. Are they trying to fix it?'

'I don't know. There were a couple of frogmen getting ready to go in as I was leaving. I'd say it's a big job.'

'Frogmen? Of course! There's a river runs down that side of that ground isn't there,' said Dixie.

'Ah "Sweet Swanwater", as the writer put it,' grinned Mr Finn.

'Yes, but there's more than that,' replied Eoin, telling them about what he had found in the book.

They were still chatting when Paddy and Sam called over to say hello.

'Were you thrilled with Eoin being the hero of the hour, Mr Madden?' Sam asked.

'Well, him and the ghosts, really,' laughed Paddy.

Eoin went red again.

'What ghosts are you talking about?' asked Dixie.

'Och, loads of them. Eoin's a total magnet for rugby-playing ghosts,' Paddy replied.

Dixie's eyes widened as Eoin stared at his feet.

'You've never mentioned this to us before,' said Mr Finn. 'Is that true?'

Eoin jumped to his feet.

'OK, look, I'm a bit wrecked by all this. I need to have a shower and change, and maybe a nap. How about we all meet down here for dinner at, say, 8.30?'

And with that he shot out of the lobby and took the stairs two at a time up to his bedroom – on the seventh floor.

He lay on his bed, still sweating, annoyed that Paddy's big mouth had revealed his biggest secret. He didn't blame his friend, but he would now have a lot of explaining to do.

A knock at the door revealed Alan, who scampered into the room bubbling with delight at the Irish victory.

'That was a brilliant win,' he gurgled, 'and what a try!'

Eoin smiled, having almost forgotten his moment of glory.

'I did up a final table for you as a, you know, souvenir.'

Written neatly on a page of his copy book was the table:

	Played	Won	Lost	Tries	Diff.	Points
Ireland	3	3	0	8	+50	12
England	3	2	1	11	+31	8
Scotland	3	1	2	6	–5	4
Wales	3	0	3	5	–76	0

Eoin smiled again. 'I will treasure this Alan, it might even turn out to be the last Ireland win at Aviva Stadium!'

Alan laughed. 'It's not that bad – is it?'

'I don't know,' Eoin replied. 'It looks like a big job, and tricky too. I'd say they will struggle to fix it in time for the Six Nations game against England.'

oin showered and got dressed as Alan watched the TV coverage of the Aviva evacuation. The reporter still hadn't found out what had happened, but spoke in a grave voice as he described how all the people who lived in the houses backing onto the stadium had now left for their own safety, and roadblocks were also in place all around the area.

'Whatever has caused the Gardaí to clear the ground has apparently come about because of a discovery by one of the Ireland Under 16 team that had just won the deciding game in the Four Nations tournament,' the TV reporter said, before cutting to some video recorded earlier. Eoin was amused, then appalled, when he saw it was Rory on the screen.

'Yeah, it was a guy from our school Castlerock,' grinned the scrum-half, who turned to the camera to say, 'Shout out to all the guys in third year!'

'And who was this hero?' asked the reporter.

'Eh, Eoin of course,' Rory replied. 'He's the guy who rescued the World Cup last year and won the Four

Nations for us today too. He's a bit of a superhero to be honest. Eoin. Eoin Madden.'

The blood drained from Eoin's face as Alan roared with laughter.

'What has he done?' moaned Eoin. 'I was hoping to keep out of the limelight for a while but now he's gone and blurted my name out on live TV and I'll be in every newspaper in the world tomorrow. I'll never be able to leave this room.'

Alan put his hand on his shoulder in sympathy, but still kept the grin on his face.

'Mr McCaffrey will be delighted at the positive publicity for the school, I suppose…'

'Oh no, that reminds me – we have that Junior Cup semi-final first thing tomorrow morning. I'll be in no state to play.'

The phone rang beside his bed. 'This is Hughie O'Farrell, *Irish Mail* newspaper,' came the voice. 'Is that Eoin Madden?'

Eoin's throat dried up. 'Yes… but I can't talk right now,' he replied, and hung up immediately.

The phone rang again. 'Tom Clifford, *Irish Examiner*…' was all Eoin heard before he clicked the button on the receiver.

He rang down to reception. 'Hi, this is Eoin in room

707, can you hold all calls for me please.'

He sat back down on the bed.

'Oh, Alan, what am I going to do? I need to go down to meet my folks for dinner but I'll be swamped.'

'Leave that with me,' his pal grinned. 'I have an idea – it's something I saw in a movie once.'

He gave Eoin his New York Yankees baseball cap and checked that he wasn't wearing any rugby kit.

Alan then slipped on one of Eoin's Ireland training jackets and left the room. 'Hang back about thirty seconds,' he ordered. 'I'll get them away from you. And use the stairs, not the lift. Wait on the first floor.'

Eoin watched as Alan walked down the corridor, pretending he was talking to someone on his phone.

'Yeah, I've been talking to Eoin,' he announced, loud enough for everyone to hear, especially the two men carrying notebooks who were standing outside the lift.

'He sneaked out the back way five minutes ago,' Alan continued into the mobile as he walked through the lift doors. 'I'm going to meet him in the pizza restaurant at Baggot Street bridge. Join us if you can, but don't say a word to any of those reporters or TV people.'

Eoin grinned as the reporters nipped into the lift just before the doors closed, and he headed down the staircase. He waited on the first floor where he was soon joined by Dixie.

'Alan has taken those chaps on a wild goose chase,' his grandfather chuckled. 'Your parents are exhausted – as am I – but while they apologise for their absence, I am more interested in finding out about you and these ghosts. There's a restaurant on this floor – hopefully they will find us a quiet corner.'

CHAPTER 36

The restaurant was almost deserted, but Dixie selected a table as far from the door as they could find, and told Eoin to sit with his back to the door. They ordered their meal and chatted about the game before Dixie changed the subject.

'Now, Eoin, I was very interested to hear your story about the ghosts,' he said once they had got settled. 'I'd love to hear more, and be quite assured that I won't think you are mad. I have even seen some myself...'

'Really?' asked Eoin. 'For a long time I thought it was just me.'

'Not at all,' replied Dixie. 'There have been tens of thousands of people who claim to have been visited by the dead. I know I have.'

Eoin cleared his throat and began. He explained how he had first come across a ghost in Lansdowne Road, the fallen rugby player Brian Hanrahan. Dixie said he remembered that name, and explained that he had once met Brian's brother Charlie.

'He was the president of the IRFU that came to visit

me when I gave up the game after… well, you know.'

Dixie's wife – Eoin's grandmother – had been killed by a falling tree branch many years before while watching Dixie play rugby. He still found it hard to talk about it.

Eoin continued, explaining the various episodes and adventures he had got up to with Brian, Dave Gallaher, Kevin Barry, Alex Obolensky and William Webb-Ellis. Dixie nodded regularly, and smiled as the story unfolded and he realised all his grandson had been up to.

Their meals arrived and they began to eat. Neither spoke for two or three minutes.

'I always wondered about that Fabergé egg thing,' Dixie smiled. 'The coincidence was too much, there had to be something else going on. You really have had some amazing experiences because you can see ghosts.'

'Yes, I suppose so,' smiled Eoin. 'It's been exciting at times – and they've been really helpful with the rugby too.'

'So, why do you think you are able to see ghosts?' asked Dixie.

Eoin shrugged. 'I really don't know, Grandad. At times, it was objects that seemed to bring them to me – like Dave Gallaher's book – but why it was me they decided to appear to I just don't understand.'

'I think I know,' the old man smiled, before wiping some food from the corner of his mouth. He paused, weighing his words.

'Eoin, you're a sensitive lad, but by that I don't mean you're some sort of wimp. You always consider other people and their feelings before your own. That's a very rare quality in a boy, or in anyone.'

Eoin looked down at his plate, embarrassed – as usual – at receiving a compliment.

'But what has that got to do with the ghosts?' he asked.

'Well… you're also an inquisitive lad, always looking to learn new things and open to new ideas. You're a loyal, solid friend to all your pals, even when they fall out with you.

'I think that there's lots of ghosts out there – maybe everyone that dies has one. Most of them never communicate with the living, but some do if they're restless, or if there's something important that needs to be done, or they have some unfinished business.'

Eoin nodded, and took another bite of his pizza. His grandfather went on.

'Look at Obolensky, or Webb-Ellis – they knew something was going on before it even happened. And Kevin Barry, he was desperate to find what happened to Eugene.'

'But why me?' asked Eoin.

'Because you are just the sort of person I'd like to help me if I came back,' he smiled. 'Brian was obviously lonely floating around Lansdowne Road all those years, he saw in you a boy from Tipperary like himself who enjoyed sport and wouldn't make a fuss. Through Brian you must have made a connection with all those other spirits – Dave was obviously delighted that someone was interested in his book after many years of it sitting there untouched. He saw a chance to do something nice for you too, and I suppose he liked the idea of keeping his memory alive.

'I think once you made that connection to the ghostly world they saw you as a friendly, welcoming link to their old lives.'

Eoin swallowed his food and smiled.

'I suppose that makes as much sense as anything,' he replied.

'Well, I think it's a good explanation,' chuckled Dixie. 'I know your grandmother has come to visit me at important moments since she passed away. She is the reason why you came to Castlerock – I suppose she's the reason why you've had all these adventures with ghosts and rugby.'

Eoin looked puzzled. 'Why's that, Grandad?'

Dixie sighed. 'Well, I explained to you before how I gave up rugby when she died, and I wouldn't let your dad play it either when he went to Castlerock.'

The old man took a sip from a glass of water and continued. 'Well, when you were coming to the end of primary school, your dad told me that he and your mother had considered sending you to boarding school but they just couldn't afford to.

'I was just about to retire from the bank – and was getting a nice sum – so I could afford to help. But I didn't want you to go away from Ormondstown… and I didn't want you to play rugby.

'Then one night your grandmother's ghost came to visit me, bright and beautiful as the day we were married. We chatted about a few things, but she told me the main reason she had come back was to ask me to help Kevin with the cost of boarding at Castlerock. She had watched you grow and thought the school would be very good for you. And she told me to encourage you to play rugby, although it took me a bit of time to come around to that.'

Eoin sat, open-mouthed, as his grandfather continued his story.

'I didn't want to tell you about the money, but I couldn't explain it all without letting you know. Anyway, the money wasn't that important, it was just that I was so moved that your grandmother – your sad, long-dead grandmother – still cared about her grandson even though he wasn't born till thirty years after she died.'

oin smiled, and finished his glass of water. The two sat in silence for several minutes, comfortable that nothing more needed to be said.

Eoin eventually broke the silence by thanking Dixie for buying him dinner.

'That was lovely – getting away from everyone especially,' he grinned. 'That's given me a lot to think about, but I'm sure I won't be doing any of that tonight – I'm only fit for sleep.'

'I'm sorry if I heaped a lot on you,' said Dixie, 'but it might make things clearer for you too. Now off you go, you've earned your sleep.'

Eoin said goodbye and took the back stairs up to his room, dodging the reporters who had returned from their fruitless chase and were back hanging around the lifts. He slipped down the corridor and into his room without being seen.

Just inside the door he spotted a note folded in two had been slipped under. He stooped to pick it up. 'Eoin. Meet me at breakfast 7.15 please,' it read. 'Lots to talk about. I'll give you and the Castlerock guys a lift to your game. Neil.'

Eoin wondered what Neil could want, as his days as an Ireland Under 16 player were now over. He recalled their conversation after the stadium evacuation, and how interested the coach was in Paddy's mention of ghosts. But before he could ponder any more, his eyelids drooped and he gave in to the losing battle with sleep.

Next morning, Eoin got up much earlier than he was used to. He dressed quietly, allowing Killian a few minutes more sleep before he woke him as he left.

'I'm going for an early breakfast, Kill. I've a game this morning so I'll be back to collect my gear. We leave here about nine.'

Eoin noticed there was no sign of the reporters at the lifts, so took the speedy way down to the ground floor. He put on a baseball cap and walked with his head down towards the dining room. He checked, but Neil had yet to arrive.

'Room number, sir?' asked the steward.

'Eh, 707,' replied Eoin.

'This way,' he said, handing him a newspaper.

As it was another matchday, Eoin ordered a light

breakfast and waited for Neil to show. He checked out the other diners in case there was any unwanted attention before he picked up and unfolded the newspaper. To his horror, his face stared back at him in a grinning photo taken when he had collected his medal the day before.

'SCHOOLBOY HERO SAVES STADIUM', read the headline, which stretched across the full width of the front page.

Eoin almost gagged on his orange juice, and quickly turned the page face down.

Neil arrived, and looked at Eoin quizzically.

'Are you OK, Eoin? You're very pale…'

'I just had a bit of a shock,' replied Eoin, turning over the newspaper to reveal his face once more.

Neil laughed. 'Oh my, that's fantastic. You're a real hero Eoin!'

Eoin frowned. 'I'm not sure I want to be. And I definitely don't want that sort of attention.'

The coach nodded, and apologised for laughing. 'It's just that you don't often see rugby on the front pages, and certainly not schoolboy players – unless it's for the wrong reasons. Don't worry, the attention will die down quickly, although you'll probably have to pose for a thousand selfies with the first years in school.'

A waiter brought Eoin's breakfast to him, and Neil ordered his own.

'Thanks for meeting me, Eoin, and thanks again for being such a brilliant player in the tournament. It's the highlight of my rugby career – although I'm sure it won't be the highlight of yours. 'The reason I asked you down was to hear about these ghosts that Paddy was talking about.'

Eoin shrugged. 'I don't really know what to say. Paddy was winding you up I think.'

'Are you sure?' Neil replied. 'I never mentioned it before, but I studied sports science in college and I did a lot of research into fatal injuries in the early days of rugby – up to about a century or so ago.

'I kept hearing stories about ghosts being seen at various grounds, but the most persistent story was about Lansdowne Road and a player who died there in 1928...'

'Brian Hanrahan,' blurted Eoin.

Neil's eyes widened.

'How did you know about him?' he asked.

Eoin lowered his eyes, chewed his lip, and looked up again at Neil.

'Because he's the ghost I met. I've met him dozens of times.'

'Really?' said Neil, his face now turning white. 'Well

161

that's extraordinary. Because he's the main reason I chose that subject to study. I heard so much about him growing up, because… well, Brian is… Brian was… my great, great-uncle.'

CHAPTER 38

t was Eoin's turn to look stunned, but the pair's expressions soon turned to grins.

'What a coincidence,' laughed Neil.

'Maybe not,' suggested Eoin. 'I've found that all the ghosts who appear to me have very good reasons for doing so.'

'All the ghosts…?' asked Neil.

Eoin sighed. 'Please Neil, please don't mention this to anyone else. I don't want people to think I'm making up things, or that I'm a bit kooky.'

He explained quickly about the various ghosts and the reasons why they had appeared to him. Neil's eyes widened as he listened, and he took a deep breath when Eoin finished his story.

'That's extraordinary, truly amazing,' he started. 'And yesterday was the first time you met Henry Dunlop?'

Eoin nodded. 'He and Brian knew there was something up with the stadium. Brian called me over after the game and that's when I found the cracks and the sinkhole.'

'It's lucky you did. Imagine if no one had noticed and the stadium was packed with over fifty thousand people for the England game next month? There could have been a huge disaster.'

Eoin gulped. 'I know. I have tickets for that stand myself for that game.'

Neil promised he wouldn't mention Eoin's story to anyone else.

'But could you do me just one favour?' he asked. 'I'd love to meet Brian. I've so much to ask him, and to tell him.'

Eoin nodded. 'I'll try. I haven't seen much of him this term, and he's usually to be found around the stadium, which is probably off-limits for a while.'

Neil nodded, and arranged to meet Eoin back in the lobby at nine o'clock.

Rory and Charlie were there before Eoin, and Paddy and Sam had come along to say goodbye and good luck.

'I don't suppose there's any chance of the grandstand collapsing at Dodder Woods, is there?' laughed Paddy.

Eoin grinned. 'Maybe your big mouth might set off a few tremors – or Rory's.'

The boys all had copies of the newspaper and jokingly asked Eoin to sign his autograph on them.

'I think they got my good side, didn't they,' chuckled Eoin. 'But any bets my Mam tells me its time I got a haircut.'

Neil arrived and helped the Castlerock trio pile their gear into the mini-van. They waved goodbye to their friends and set off on the road to Dodder, a boarding school twenty miles outside the city.

Eoin was relieved to be out of the hotel and away from the new pressures that had come after the tournament was over. It would be good to be back with his school mates.

The journey went quickly, with Rory keeping everyone entertained with his stories about how he and Alan had fooled the reporters the night before by taking them on a wild goose chase around the restaurants of the area.

Alan was waiting in the car park when they pulled into Dodder Woods.

'Hey, Eoin, did you see the paper?' he called as the players stepped out of the van.

Eoin lifted his gear out onto the ground, and turned to his pal.

'Hi Alan. Thanks again for your help last night, and yes, I've seen the papers. Has anyone else in Castlerock?'

'Eh… yes,' he replied, pointing to where the team had gathered outside the dressing room and were now waving newspapers at him and chanting, 'He-rohhh, he-rohhh, he-ro-ohhh'.

Eoin waved back, jokingly soaking up the adulation, but noticed that just one of the team was standing off to one side, not taking part in the fun.

Dylan.

CHAPTER 39

'All right everyone, time to get changed,' called out Mr Carey, who pointed them in the direction of the dressing rooms.

Eoin, Rory and Charlie followed the rest of the squad inside, taking the bench in the corner before the coach began his talk. Eoin tried to catch Dylan's eye, but the Castlerock captain didn't seem to want to have anything to do with him.

Mr Carey welcomed the international trio back, and reminded them of the Castlerock tactical calls and how they would have to quickly forget they were playing for Ireland. Dylan said a few words too, but didn't mention the returnees.

Outside, Eoin nodded to Dodder Woods' Oisín Deegan, who less than twenty-four hours before had been his team-mate. He also exchanged a glance with Marcus McCord, who he had played with for Leinster before the second-row was discarded. The fact that he was a bully and had cheated his way on to the team didn't endear him to Eoin, or anyone else.

Having played at a higher level for weeks, Eoin found it very easy to adjust to Junior Cup schools' rugby. He and Rory were in top form, and their interplay set up two tries for the centres, Richie and Mikey, in the first ten minutes. With a couple of minutes left in the half Eoin sent up a garryowen, and chased it all the way into the Dodder 22.

He fielded the ball before it bounced, and although he fell heavily he fed the ball back quickly and Castlerock continued to attack. He had just stood up when he heard another cheer as the replacement winger, Theo Phelan, crossed for a try.

'Nineteen-nil,' grinned Mr Carey at half-time as the energy bars and bottles of orange were passed around. 'I think we can make a few changes now. We don't want to flog our best players with the final coming so soon.'

Eoin glanced across at Rory, who looked just as puzzled as he was.

'Grehan and Madden, we'll take you off. Duffy into out-half, Joe Memery comes on at centre and Charlie Adams at No.9.'

There was general surprise among the squad, who had become used to having Eoin there to solve all their problems when they arose. But Mr Carey reassured them that there was enough talent still there to not just hold on but to extend their lead.

Eoin wasn't so sure of that, but he didn't say anything out loud. He bit his tongue again when Dodder scored a try with the first attack of the second half. Castlerock were no longer the smooth-running assured half-back unit that had been seen in the first half. Duffy wasn't a bad player, but he didn't have Eoin's eye for a gap or willingness to do something a bit different. Dodder soon saw the predictability in his play and moved to close him down. Duffy then started to get ratty and blamed Charlie Adams for his own mistakes.

The result of all this proved disastrous, and within twenty minutes the 19-0 half-time lead was down to 19-17.

Mr Carey changed the whole front row, and when Theo Phelan was knocked flat by a heavy tackle he was forced to send on Shane Keane, who hadn't played all season due to injury.

'I've no one left on the bench,' he sighed. 'We can't afford anyone else to get injured.'

Eoin and Rory looked at each other again, despairing at what was happening out on the field and seeing their hopes of a second Junior Cup medal slipping away.

Castlerock battled hard, but it was clear they were going to crack at some stage. Charlie Bermingham was magnificent, tackling everything that moved within five metres of him, but the toll of playing nearly three hours of rugby in less than twenty hours was starting to tell.

What made matters worse was Richie Duffy's goal kicking – Castlerock had been lucky to receive two penalties from kickable distance, but both were badly skewed well wide of the posts.

And then to cap it all, Joe Memery was the victim of a crunching tackle that left him out cold on the ground. The coaches and match officials stood around as he was helped to his feet by the school doctor, who told the referee he would have to do a head injury assessment.

Mr Carey walked back to the touchline and shrugged his shoulders.

'Whatever chance we had of holding on with fifteen men, we've none with fourteen,' he muttered to Eoin and Rory.

They watched as Joe was helped from the field, knowing that whatever the result of the head injury assessment, as a youth player he would not be allowed on the field again.

'Mr Carey, Mr Carey,' came a call from behind the bench where the Castlerock team were sitting. Through the crowd pushed Alan, waving a booklet.

'Mr Carey,' he gasped. 'You know you can put back

on someone you've already substituted?'

'What? How?' asked the puzzled coach.

'Look, it's here in the laws,' replied Alan. '3.14, Substituted players rejoining the match. "A player can come back to replace a player undertaking a Head Injury Assessment in accordance with Law 3.12",' he read. 'That means you can bring Eoin back on… or anyone else, of course.'

Mr Carey snatched the laws book from Alan's hand and raced across to where the referee was about the restart the game.

Eoin and his pals watched as Mr Carey animatedly explained the situation, stabbing his finger in the booklet. The Dodder coach joined them, but after a few seconds they all seemed to agree and Mr Carey raced back to the touchline.

'Madden, get your tracksuit off. You're going out-half of course, tell Duffy to drop back to centre. And Eoin… win this game for us.

'And Alan, you little beauty. If we win the cup I'll make sure you get a medal.'

CHAPTER 40

There was just over ten minutes left, but Eoin's arrival had given Castlerock a huge boost. There was a new spring in their step, and every player tackled just that little bit harder.

Eoin took control in midfield and ensured Dodder never got a chance to make a scoring chance. With the clock ticking into the last minute they grew desperate and Eoin noticed the scrum-half was shaping to try a skip pass which might release their backs. Just as he got the ball away Eoin charged for the gap and was delighted he had read the plan. Instead of the ball ending up in Marcus McCord's hands, Eoin snatched it out of the air and sprinted out of reach of the defence.

As he neared the goalposts he looked over his shoulder, but Dodder Woods' defence had already given up the chase. The only player there to usher him home was Dylan, a rare grin on his face.

'Ah Dyl, you're always there in support, no matter what,' smiled Eoin. 'Here, you deserve this,' he added, tossing the ball back to his pal who returned the grin before touching the ball down under the crossbar.

The pair were instantly submerged in a sea of Castlerock jerseys, but Eoin shook off the attention to prepare himself for the conversion. It went over easily, and he rejoined his delighted team-mates on the sideline.

Mr Carey spoke first: 'Right lads, that was a close one, and I apologise for mishandling the replacements. But Alan was on top of the regulations and we owe him a huge debt. Now, take it easy this weekend – the final is only five days away and we don't need any more injury doubts.'

Eoin put his arm across Alan's shoulder as they walked off the field.

'That was some stunt, Al. Do you read those rule books in bed at night?'

'Sometimes,' admitted his friend. 'Somebody has to know the rules properly – and didn't it pay off today?'

'Totally,' laughed Eoin.

Dylan jogged up alongside and he too thanked Alan.

'And you too,' he grinned at Eoin. 'I must confess I was glad to see you coming back on. And fair play for handing me that try.'

'No bother, how many is that now in the cup run?'

'Twelve,' replied Dylan. 'Mr Finn says he's been checking back through the school archives and thinks it might even be close to the record for the whole competition.'

'Cool,' said Alan. 'I'll ask Mr Finn if he needs a hand. We'd be a lot quicker with a computer.'

CHAPTER 41

The bus pulled into the Castlerock car park in late afternoon, when there was a large group of boarders waiting to welcome them.

'Another final,' called out Mr McCaffrey as Dylan led his team off the bus to load applause and cheers.

As Eoin got off he was greeted by a series of clicks as if a busload of grasshoppers had just pulled up too. He stared out at his fellow pupils, most of whom were pointing smart phone cameras at him, and he just knew he would be all over social media within a few minutes.

Mr McCaffrey must have sensed his discomfort, because he bellowed at the boys to stop.

'Right,' he roared. 'I want a queue to form in front of me, and I want to see everyone who took a photo of any of this team deleting it. This is private property and your schoolmates are entitled to privacy here. If I see any evidence of such photos appearing on interweb sites I will be calling your parents, confiscating your phone and computer, and barring you from any extra-curricular activities for a month.'

The boys gasped, and hurried to form a line in front of the headmaster.

'Just because one of our pupils has attracted some degree of celebrity does not allow you to invade his privacy. He has a big game ahead, and his Junior Certificate examination, so please leave him in peace.'

Eoin sighed with relief, and nodded his thanks to the headmaster.

'There's been a couple of journalists knocking around,' Mr Carey told him. 'But Mr McCaffrey gave them the fright of their lives. He took down that cavalry sword from over his mantelpiece and took it out to the front of the school where he waved it over his head. They took to their heels and ran!'

Eoin laughed, picturing Mr McCaffrey as a type of Braveheart-in-a-suit, and himself, Dylan and Alan chuckled all the way up to their dormitory.

Eoin kept his head down for the next three days, desperately trying to catch up with the studies which he had neglected as rugby took charge. He kept up his exercising too, and he treasured the twenty-minute jog he took to start and finish his day.

The night before the final he headed off in the direction of The Rock, halting his stopwatch as he made his way through the bushes. Twilight had fallen, and the orange glow in the sky reminded him of home as he sat and relaxed his leg muscles.

As he sipped from a bottle of water he heard the familiar rustling which heralded the arrival of one of his spectral friends. Looking around, he was surprised to see that it was the newest ghost in his life, Henry Dunlop, who had appeared.

'Ah, Master Madden, we meet again. Mr Hanrahan told me that I would find you here.'

Eoin greeted the elderly gentleman, who was wearing a shiny black silk top hat.

'We – the rugby spirits – have all been very shocked by that has happened to the old Champion Club ground…'

Eoin looked puzzled, but remembered from his book that that was the name of the first club to occupy Lansdowne Road.

'Ah, the Aviva,' he said.

'Yes, that strange glass and steel box where once we had a covered shed and a rope to keep spectators from walking onto the pitch.'

'I don't think a rope would work these days,' grinned Eoin.

'Indeed,' said Henry, returning the smile.

'The rest of them are back at the ground, helping to guide the engineers to the dangerous parts, although they don't really know they are being guided. It's lucky you arrived when you did, as I think the next big game could have caused a serious collapse. We hear them discussing the problems and it now appears there will be no need for demolition, just some excavation to redirect the old streams and repair work. They'll be testing it for months to make sure it's safe though.'

'So, they won't be playing England there next month?' asked Eoin.

'No, I think they said they would play it somewhere else in Dublin. Cork Park, I think they called it?'

Eoin laughed at Henry, and corrected him, before he made his farewells and jogged back to the dormitory.

CHAPTER 42

The Junior Cup final was usually staged in Aviva Stadium, but had been moved at very short notice to the Leinster stadium in Donnybrook village. Although the occasion seemed smaller, Eoin liked the little ground, which would be packed to the rafters for the final. It was even more special for him because the opponents were Rostipp College, a school not far from his home where several of his primary school friends were now studying.

That meant that every second accent he heard as he walked around the ground was a Tipperary one. Because of his local connections and the recent publicity, most of the opposing fans knew who he was and they unleashed plenty of light-hearted banter in his direction.

Eoin hated the attention, and got through his pre-match routines as quickly as possible. Back in the dressing room, Mr Carey handed the team sheet to the stadium announcer and turned to talk to his team.

'This will be a tough, physical game, so be ready for them. They'll come at you from the first whistle. Let's get the ball quickly to Eoin, and use our extra pace. Alan has showed me some of the videos of their games and their full back is dodgy if you put him under pressure from high kicks.'

Alan smiled in the corner as everyone grinned at him.

'Any other observations, Mr Analyst?' asked the coach.

'The Savage brothers have won 98 per cent of all Rostipp line-outs this season, so it's easy enough to know what to do there.

'And oh yeah, Mr Finn and I have been digging back into the archives and Dylan has a chance of breaking the Leinster Junior Cup try-scoring record today. He has twelve already and the record is thirteen – by an old Castlerock guy called Dixie Madden. Eoin's grandad.'

Eoin tried hard not to look annoyed. It wasn't that it was Dixie whose record was in danger, but he feared that Dylan would let the pursuit of the landmark get in the way of the most important target today – winning the cup.

There was a ripple of wows and good-lucks but Mr Carey seemed to share Eoin's misgivings.

'Alright, alright, settle down. I'm sure we'd all be delighted if Dylan was to break the record, but I'd be much, much happier if you were all sitting here two hours from now with a gold medal hanging from your neck. Rugby is a team game and I'm sure Dylan won't let you forget that too.'

Mr Carey was right about Rostipp, whose forwards looked five centimetres taller and five kilograms heavier than Castlerock's. From the kick-off they charged at their opponents' pack, with pursuit of the ball low down on their list of priorities.

Charlie Bermingham took a huge blow as two Rostipp players arrived at once, and the Castlerock back-row fell awkwardly on his shoulder. His cries alerted the referee to bring play to a halt.

'I heard it pop ref,' Charlie winced. 'I'll need the doc.'

The referee called on the medical officer who took one look at Charlie and signalled to Mr Carey that his part in the game was now over. With help from the referee he lifted Charlie to his feet and they shouldered him from the field.

As the official jogged back onto the field he was confronted by Dylan.

'What are you going to do about that, ref?' Dylan asked. 'That was pure thuggery? Charlie was nowhere near the ball – they just took him out.'

The referee seemed taken aback at having to stoop so the smallest man on the field could berate him, but he waved the Castlerock skipper away.

'Knock-on, scrum to Rostipp,' he called.

The decision almost caused Dylan to explode, but Eoin signalled to him to keep his mouth shut.

Rostipp won the scrum, and used their physical advantage to advance up the field play by play, metre by metre. Eoin looked across to Dylan, who shrugged his shoulders. Castlerock were getting pulverized, they needed to get the ball out of the forward battle and hope they got a bit of luck.

Their need for a bit of luck increased as Rostipp's pressure led to a rolling maul which rolled right up to the Castlerock line with embarrassing ease. The No. 8 peeled off the back and touched down for the opening score.

'We're getting murdered up front, and the ref's too soft on them,' grumbled Rory.

'Forget the ref, there's nothing we can do about that,' snapped Eoin. 'Let's get the ball away from the forwards as much as we can and tackle everything that moves. If we keep them frustrated they'll give away penalties and I'll bet they fade in the last ten.'

Eoin knew that was easier said than done, but he also

knew it was important to change things before Castlerock were swamped. The Rostipp back line was slow,
but they tackled hard too and Eoin grew frustrated
trying to break through their defence. The game became
bogged down in the middle of the field and when the
teams left for the half-time some spectators began whis-
tling in complaint at the boredom.

'Don't worry about that,' grinned Eoin as he and
Dylan walked off. 'We'll have the crowd asleep by the
last ten minutes – and then we'll strike.'

CHAPTER 43

The second half continued as the first had ended, and Rostipp's players *did* start to get annoyed. Whatever their coach had said to them at half-time wasn't working, and they began to make silly errors. Eoin punished them from the kicking tee, so by half way through the second period Castlerock had brought the margin down to a single point, with the score standing at 7-6.

'This is working,' Dylan muttered as Eoin took a breather while Rostipp made a couple of substitutions.

'Maybe,' replied Eoin. 'But our guys have taken an awful lot of punishment. We need to just keep going. Carey needs to bring on two new props though. The O'Sullivan brothers are strong and fit, just what we need right now.' Dylan signalled to the coach, who seemed to agree because the substitution was made at the next break in play.

Jimmy and Archie were not the best props in the squad, but they were the bravest, most willing tacklers and their arrival proved a shock to Rostipp. In every attack the O'Sullivans were first to the ball-carrier and their power meant they floored the Rostippers.

Castlerock began to get more confidence in the scrum too, and when they won one against the head there was a huge roar from their supporters. With the Rostipp defence on the wrong foot, Rory went on a run that evaded three tacklers and took Castlerock into the 22.

Eoin put his hand on the ball at the back of the ruck and looked around. He spotted a gap down the side of the ruck and went for it, bringing the ball to ten metres from the posts.

He whispered into Rory's ear: 'I'm dropping back, give it to my right,' before rushing back behind the centres. Rory zipped the ball back as Eoin had asked and the out-half had the extra tenth of a second he needed. He swung his boot back and connected perfectly just as the ball met the ground. It flew high and straight, soaring high above the posts underneath which the referee raised his left arm and blew his whistle.

Eoin got a few pats on the back for his three-pointer but hurried his team-mates back into their positions. The game still hung on a knife edge and he knew Rostipp had enough talent and power to get a winning score.

The Tipperary side were shocked at the scoreboard reverse and came back strongly – but Castlerock held firm. Dylan battled as hard as anyone else, putting his tiny body on the line.

With time running out Rostipp grew increasingly desperate and began taking risky moves. Eoin had always been aware of the chances of an interception, but he chose his moment perfectly. Roger Savage was tackled just outside the Castlerock 22 but without immediate support he looked to offload while off balance. Eoin swooped and snatched the ball from the air, dodged a tackle and set off down the field.

The full-back moved to tackle him, but Eoin saw Dylan coming up fast behind him and slipped him the ball. The winger was off free and made a dash for the posts alone, but as he reached them he turned and fired the ball back to Eoin.

'But… the record,' gasped Eoin.

'Score!' insisted Dylan, and Eoin touched the ball down.

The pair were instantly buried by a mountain of Castlerock team-mates – and one or two excited supporters – but Eoin shook them all off and prepared to take the conversion.

'No pressure lad, this is the last kick,' grinned the ref. 'Just get it over and we can all go home.'

Eoin grinned back at him and took a glance towards

the stand where his mum, dad and Dixie waved back at him. He looked up at the sky, savouring the moment, before he took aim and slotted the ball neatly between the uprights.

Again he became submerged in sweaty team-mates and collected a full set of hugs before the squad made its way in front of the grandstand. The stadium announcer called out the names of the beaten side who collected their medals before he began reading out the Castlerock team-sheet.

Eoin collected his shiny slice of metal and watched his team-mates collect theirs one by one before the replacements came up. 'O'Sullivan, O'Sullivan, Phelan, Adams, Memery…' went the announcer, building up to the climax when he would announce '… and the victorious captain, Dylan Coonan.'

But there was an extra name, which came just before Dylan's: 'analyst Alan Handy' the announcer called, to loud cheers from the crowd and complete bewilderment from Alan who was not expecting to be honoured. Eoin cheered as Alan – his face by now bright red – collected his medal and hung it around his neck.

That left just one more presentation, and Dylan stepped forward and lifted the silver trophy high above his head, thrusting it into the air four times while the

Castlerock supporters cheered. They continued showing their appreciation as Dylan led his players on a lap
of honour, with each player getting a few seconds to
carry the cup.

'What were you doing giving away that try at the
end,' asked Eoin, as he jogged alongside his friend.

'Ah, sure as you said it's a team game. And I'm
delighted to have played my part in our team winning
it. You deserved the try more than anyone, and I would
have felt terrible taking the record away from Dixie,
who was a better player than I'll ever be.'

'I'm sure he wouldn't have minded,' grinned Eoin,
'but thanks, anyway. It was a lovely thing to do.'

CHAPTER 44

The winning Junior Cup team didn't have long to rest on their laurels, as they were all reminded the following morning just how close the state exams were.

'Now we're all very grateful for your extraordinary victory yesterday,' beamed Mr McCaffrey as the squad enjoyed a special breakfast in the staff dining room. 'And your names will go down in the annals of Castlerock.

'However, your parents and guardians have sent you here not just to play rugby football, but also to secure a good education – which means performing as well in the Junior Cert as you have in the Junior Cup.

'And as you have sacrificed plenty of study time to sport over recent weeks, I expect to see you all redouble your efforts in the run into the exams.'

Dylan winked at Eoin. 'No problem to you Eoin, I know you've been doing some sneaky study on the side.'

Eoin winced. 'I wish. No, it's hard work from here on – except for next Saturday of course.'

With Aviva Stadium out of commission, Ireland's Six Nations fixture against England had been switched to the GAA stadium at Croke Park, and Eoin had some precious extra tickets for the game. As a thank you for what it called his heroism, the IRFU had invited Eoin to bring his entire family, friends and team-mates for lunch and to watch the game from a private box.

Even Richie Duffy was being friendly, although Eoin had already decided that he would be taking every member of the squad along. He had a few spare seats, and decided to invite some of his fellow members of the Ireland squad too.

It was raining on the morning of the game, but Eoin still went out for his jog around the grounds before breakfast. It has been a couple of weeks since he had taken a detour to The Rock, but today he felt the need for a short breather. Slipping into the little haven he was struck by how bright it was, and how loud the tiny stream sounded as the water bubbled over the rocks. But in every other way it was peaceful, with no sign of life – or of after-life.

Eoin relaxed, taking a rare moment to himself to reflect on what he was going to do that day. He wondered about the ghosts who used to visit him there, but he had sense or feeling that they were not around anymore. If that was so, he would miss them, especially Brian, but he knew too that they needed their peace.

CHAPTER 45

Croke Park was much bigger than Aviva Stadium, but the IRFU had no problem selling the extra seats, even at short notice. The roar that greeted the teams sent a shiver up Eoin's spine, and he turned and grinned at Dixie sitting beside him in the viewing box.

'This is an amazing ground, isn't it?' said his grandfather. 'I would have loved to have played here.'

The game was a tense, tight affair, as was expected with both sides looking to complete a rare Grand Slam after each had won their previous four games. At half-time he slipped back into the area of the box where there were refreshments for the guests. He asked for a cola and chatted about the game to Paddy and Sam.

'The referee's brutal,' complained Paddy, whose father Simon laughed.

'Every referee is brutal according to you,' he chuckled. 'I think he's doing a decent job.'

Eoin nodded and reminded his pal how he had complained about all the officials in all the tournaments they had ever played in.

As they were chatting, a knock came to the door of the box, and the steward who answered called out Eoin's name.

Standing outside in the hallway was Neil.

'How are you Eoin,' he grinned. 'Enjoying the hospitality of the Union I hope?'

'We are indeed,' replied Eoin. 'It's a lovely day so far – just need the result to go our way and it will be perfect.'

Neil paused and looked up and down the corridor.

'I was wondering… have you seen Brian lately?' he asked, looking at the floor.

Eoin shrugged. 'I've been looking but there's no sign of him in his usual haunts. I haven't been able to get into the Aviva of course.'

'Yes, I understand. Although I heard today they've almost completed the work and it will be open again for the soccer internationals in June.'

'That's great news,' said Eoin. 'But I hope we don't have to wait that long to see Brian.'

'True. I must confess I've been thinking about it a lot since you told me. It's a huge part of my family's story… I hope I get to see him soon.'

Eoin said goodbye and slipped back into the box where he went around to check that all his guests were having fun.

For the second-half he sat with Alan and Dylan, and the trio enjoyed spotting the tactical moves develop and anticipating what might happen next. Alan had his notebook with him and scribbled notes at every opportunity.

'I'm not sure there's enough work as an analyst,' he announced at one stage. 'So, I might do a coaching course instead.'

Dylan and Eoin chuckled, but made sure to agree with their pal. 'You'd be a brilliant coach,' enthused Dylan.

They cheered as Ireland took the lead with their fourth penalty goal but England hit back immediately with a well-worked try. With five minutes left they still held the advantage, although Ireland were attacking inside their 22.

A line-out was being formed in the far corner of the ground, close to the terraces on Hill Sixteen, when Eoin spotted a familiar red, black and gold jersey among the replacements who were running along the touchline to follow the play.

'There's Brian!' he gasped, pointing him out to Dylan and Alan, before checking that nobody else had heard him.

'What's he up to?' asked Alan.

'Is there another guy over there with him?' asked Dylan.

194

Eoin stared closely and reckoned Dylan was right. Another player in old fashioned long shorts and a green jumper was standing alongside Brian. They seemed to be pointing at the players and making suggestions about the game, although nobody seemed to be listening.

Ireland took a long throw from the line-out, and the powerful centre picked up the loose ball and crashed through a couple of tackles before he was brought down close to the line. Eoin and his friends – and most of the 82,000 spectators – were on their feet roaring as the ruck was contested. After a few seconds, the ball squirted out on the Irish side and was gathered by the scrum-half. He had half a second to decide but opted to dive straight for the tiny gap in the enormous defence.

He made it, grounding the ball before he was crushed by a mountain of players, but rose again moments later with a huge grin on his face. Eoin hugged Dylan as everyone dressed in green in the ground danced a jig of delight.

The final whistle soon blew and more joy spread across the stadium. Being the last game of the season, a trophy presentation was required and a team of workers soon assembled the platform in the middle of the pitch.

As the Castlerock boys watched, another man came to the door of their box and asked for Eoin. It was the

IRFU official he had first told about the damage to the Aviva Stadium.

'Eoin, my boss told me to come over here and give you these,' he started, handing him three plastic badges hanging from green ribbons. 'This is a historic occasion and it has gone off without a hitch, even the result was right. You played a huge part in ensuring this was the case, and these badges will get you on to the pitch below for the celebrations. Go down there and meet your heroes, and enjoy the fun.'

Eoin's eyes widened, and after he had thanked the man, he rushed back to tell Dylan and Alan he wanted them to come with him. The boys could barely keep from screaming with delight as they passed through the various checkpoints waving the precious passes.

Out on the field, they were in time to see the Six Nations trophy being handed over, and the fireworks exploding into the night sky. The first flash lit up the field and he spotted Neil standing on the touchline in his IRFU tracksuit.

'Hey Neil, how did you get out here?' laughed Alan.

'Ah, they were keeping me in reserve in case the head coach got food poisoning' he replied, with a big grin on his face. 'I see you got some top notch passes there.'

The boys wandered around, but kept away from the

players who were enjoying their deserved victory. Eoin spotted Brian again, and ran back to find Neil.

'Come with me quickly,' he said, ushering him down towards the Hill end. 'Can you see anything?' he asked Neil, as he pointed to where Brian seemed to be playing football with the other figure.

'Not a thing. Is Brian down here?'

Eoin called out to his ghostly pal, who stopped and turned.

'Eoin, how are you? That was some finish to the game, wasn't it?'

'It was,' he agreed. 'It was an amazing win.'

He explained to Brian that the man standing ten metres away was the Under 16 coach, and that he really wanted to meet him.

Brian shrugged his shoulders. 'I don't really get to choose who I meet,' he explained. 'You were the first for many years, although I know some of your chums were able to see me too. Who is this man, Neil?'

Eoin called Neil over, and introduced them to each other, but frustratingly they were unable to connect.

'I can't see anything Eoin,' sighed Neil.

'I can see him though,' said Brian. 'And the other 80,000 people staring down at us right now. Why does he want to see me?'

Eoin looked Brian in the eye. 'Because he's your great, great nephew,' he told him.

Brian's face crumpled, and he reached out to the coach. Whatever passed between them, Neil suddenly seemed to react and threw his own arms out for a hug. It must have looked a bit odd to whichever of the spectators happened to look their way, but Eoin, Neil and Brian didn't care. Tears flowed from the two men as they connected across the decades.

'We've a lot to talk about,' said Neil, staring at the long-dead rugby player. 'Let's go find a quiet corner.'

The pair walked away side by side, leaving Eoin, Alan and Dylan open-mouthed at what they had just witnessed. Eoin realised the man who had been kicking ball with Brian was still there, and asked him how he had got there.

'I'm a ghost too,' he grinned. 'I recognised a kindred spirit in Brian – and his Tipperary accent too. I hear a bit of one in you too, where are you from?'

'Ormondstown,' Eoin told him, 'in the north of the county.'

'Ah, I'm from down the other end, near Kilkenny,' he replied. 'Grangemockler it's called.'

'And what are you doing here?' asked Eoin.

'Ah, well I've something else in common with Brian,

I suppose,' replied the man. 'This is the place I died too – they even named a stand after me here. My name is Hogan, Michael Hogan. But that's another story.'

AUTHOR'S NOTE

Sheepishly, I must confess that I co-wrote (with Malachy Clerkin) the history of Lansdowne Road that Eoin gets for Christmas (*Lansdowne Road: The Stadium; the matches; the greatest days*, Malachy Clerkin and Gerard Siggins, The O'Brien Press). And as Alan and Eoin discover, there were indeed two small streams that once ran underneath what is now Aviva Stadium. However, the new stadium was built to the highest standards and there is no chance of a sink hole developing, such as I wrote in this novel.

The book also tells more of the life of Henry Dunlop, the interesting man whose vision and drive ensured we have a wonderful sports ground beside the River Dodder.

RUGBY SPIRIT

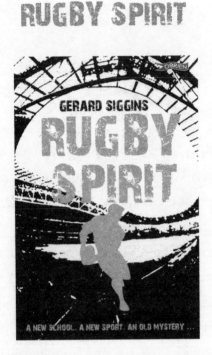

A new school. A new sport. An old mystery...

Eoin's has just started a new school ... and a new sport. Everyone at school is mad about rugby, but Eoin hasn't even held a rugby ball before! And why does everybody seem to know more about his own grandad than he does?

RUGBY WARRIOR

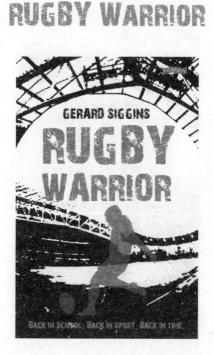

Back in school. Back in sport. Back in time.

Eoin Madden is now captain of the Under 14s team and has to deal with friction between his friend Rory and new boy Dylan as they battle for a place as scrum-half. Fast-paced action, mysterious spirits and feuding friends – it's a season to remember!

RUGBY REBEL

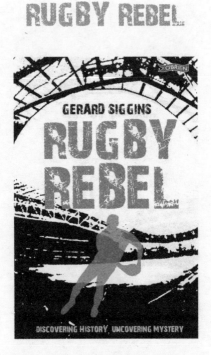

Discovering History. Uncovering Mystery

Eoin Madden's been moved up to train with the Junior Cup team, which is hard work, plus there's trouble in school as mobile phones start going missing! But there are ghostly goings-on in Castlerock – what's the link between Eoin's history lessons and the new spirit he's spotted wearing a Belvedere rugby jersey?

RUGBY FLYER

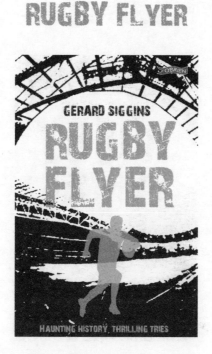

Haunting history. Thrilling tries.

Eoin and his new friends are taken on a trip to Twickenham to play & watch rugby. There, he meets a ghost: Prince Obolensky, a Russian who played rugby for England, scored a world famous try against New Zealand in Twickenham and later joined the RAF and died in WW2.

RUGBY RUNNER

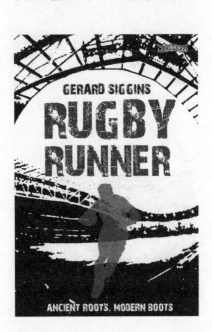

Ancient Roots. Modern boots.

Eoin Madden is captain of the Junior Cup team, training with Leinster and aiming for Ireland's Under 16 World Cup team. He also has to deal with grumpy friends, teachers piling on the homework – AND a ghost on a mission that goes back to the very origins of the game of rugby.